The Deep Lake Mystery

Carolyn Wells

The Deep Lake Mystery

The present edition is a reproduction of previous publication of this classic work. Minor typographical errors may have been corrected without note; however, for an authentic reading experience the spelling, punctuation, and capitalization have been retained from the original text.

ISBN: 978-1-63637-840-4

CONTENTS

CHAPTER I

"A STATELY PLEASURE DOME ..."

As I look back on my life, eventful enough in spots, but placid, even monotonous in the long stretches between spots, I think the greatest thrill I ever experienced was when I saw the dead body of Sampson Tracy.

Imagine to yourself a man, dead in his own bed, with no sign of violence or maltreatment. Eyes partly closed, as he might be peacefully thinking, and no expression of fear or horror on his calm face.

Now add to your mental picture the fact that he had round his brow a few flowers arranged as a wreath. More flowers diagonally across his breast, like a garland. Clasped in his right hand, against his heart, an ivory crucifix, and in his left hand an orange.

Sticking up from behind his head showed the plume of a red feather duster!

And draped round all this, like a frame, was a red chiffon scarf, a filmy but voluminous affair, deftly tucked in here and there, and encircling all the strange and bizarre details I have enumerated.

On a pillow, near the dead face, lay two small crackers and a clean, folded handkerchief.

As I stared, my imagination flew to the Indians or the ancient Egyptians, who provided their dead with food and toilet implements, which were buried with them.

But in this case——

I believe it was Abraham Lincoln who said: "If you have a story to tell, begin at the beginning, go through with the tale, and leave off at the ending." So, as I most assuredly have a story to tell, I will begin at the beginning and follow the prescribed directions.

It all began, I suppose, the night Keeley Moore came to see me about fishing tackle. Kee is a wonderful detective and all that, but when it comes to fishing he's mighty glad to ask my advice.

And Lord knows I'm glad to give it to him.

We used to go fishing together, every summer. Then Kee took it into his silly head to get married, and to a girl who cares nothing about fishing.

So from that you can see how things are.

But this time Kee seemed really excited about his prospects of fishing through the summer months.

"We're going to Wisconsin," he told me, with a note of

joyousness in his voice, "and, Gray, do you know, there are more than two thousand lakes in one county out in that foolish old state?"

"I'd like to fish in all of 'em," I said, with my usual lack of moderation.

"You can't do that, but you can fish in a few, if you like. Lora sends you, and I back it up, an invitation to come out there as soon as we get settled and stay as long as you can."

"That's a tempting bid," I told him, "but I can't impose on newlyweds like that. I'll go to the inn or lodge or whatever they have out there, and see you every day."

"No, we want you with us. We've taken a fairly good-sized house for the season, and you must be our guest. Lora's asking a few of her friends and I want you."

Well, he had little trouble in persuading me, once I felt convinced that his wife's invitation was in good faith, and I planned to go out there early in August.

They were going in July, which left them time enough to get settled and get their home in running order.

So I went to Wisconsin in August, glad enough to get away from the city's heat and noise and dirt.

Deep Lake, the choice of the Moores, was in Oneida County, which is designated among the Scenic Sections of Wisconsin as North Woods—Eastern.

And scenic it surely was. The last part of the train ride had shown me that, and when we were motoring from the railroad station to the Moore bungalow, I was impressed with the weird beauty all about.

It was dusk, and the tall trees looked black against the sky. Long shadows of hemlocks and poplars fell across the road, as the last glow of the sunset was fading, and the reflection in the lakes of surrounding scenery was clear, though dark and eerie-looking.

We passed several lakes before we reached the journey's end.

"Here we are!" Moore cried at last, as we turned in at the gates of a most attractive estate.

A short road led to the front door and Lora came out to greet us.

I liked Kee Moore's wife, though I never felt I knew her very well. She was of a reserved type and while amiable and cordial, she was not responsive and never seemed to offer or invite confidence.

But she greeted me heartily, and expressed real pleasure at having me there.

She was very good looking—a wholesome, bonny type, with an air of executive ability and absolute savoir faire.

Her hair was dead gold, bobbed and worn straight, I think they call it a Dutch bob. Anyway, she had a trace of Dutch effect and reminded me of that early picture of Queen Wilhelmina.

She sent me to my room to brush up but told me I needn't change as the bungalow was run informally.

The place rejoiced in the name of "Variable Winds," and though the Moores guyed the idea of having a name for such an unpretentious affair, they admitted it was at least appropriate.

I returned to the living room to find the group augmented by a few more people: one house guest and two or three neighbours.

Cocktails appeared and the cheery atmosphere dispelled the darksome and gloomy effects that had marked our drive from the station.

I found myself next my fellow guest, a pleasant-faced lady, who introduced herself.

"I'm Maud Merrill," she vouchsafed. "I'm staying here, so you must learn to like me."

"No trouble at all," I told her, and honestly, for I liked her at once.

She was a widow, perhaps thirty or so, with white hair and deep blue eyes. I judged her hair was prematurely grayed, for her face was young and attractive.

"I'm an old schoolmate of Lora Moore's," she disclosed further, "and I'm up here for a fortnight. Are you staying long?"

"I'm invited indefinitely," I returned. "I'll stay a month, I think, if they seem to want me."

"Oh, they will. They've both looked forward to your coming with real delight. And you'll like it here. There's no end of things to do. Fishing of course, and bathing and boating and golf and tennis and dancing and flirting—in fact, you can have just whatever sport you want."

"Sounds rather strenuous. I had hoped for a restful time."

"Yes, you can have that if you really want it. Let me give you a hint of the other guests. The beautiful woman is Katherine Dallas. She's about to be married to our next-door neighbour. He isn't here to-night. But one of his house guests is here. That tall, thin man,—he's Harper Ames."

I thanked her for her hints, though I wasn't terribly interested. But it's good to know a little about new acquaintances, and often prevents unfortunate speeches. Especially with me. For I've a shocking habit of saying the wrong thing and making enemies thereby.

At the table I found myself seated at my hostess's right hand and the beautiful Mrs. Dallas on my other side.

It was a comfortable sort of party. The conversation, while not specially brilliant, was unforced and gayly bantering. Two youngsters were present, who added their flapper slang to the general fund of amusement.

These two were Posy May and Dick Hardy, and though apparently about twenty they seemed to have world-wide knowledge and world-old wisdom.

"My canoe upset this afternoon," Posy told the company with an air of being a heroine.

"You upset it on purpose," declared Dick.

"Didn't, either. I turned around too quickly——"

"Yes, and if I hadn't been on the job you'd be turning around there yet."

"Posy," Keeley said, reproachfully, "you must be more careful. Deep Lake is one of the deepest and most treacherous lakes in all Wisconsin. Now, don't cut up silly tricks in a canoe."

"Oh, I know how to manage a canoe."

"You managed to upset," said Lora Moore, accusingly, and pretty Posy changed the subject.

After dinner there was a little bridge, but the youngsters were going to a dance, and Mrs. Dallas seemed to want to go home early, so Ames carried her off, and our own quartet was left alone.

I was glad of it, for I like a chat with a few better than the rattle of the crowd. And it was not very long before Lora and Mrs. Merrill left us, and Keeley and I had the porch to ourselves.

"Pleasant people," I said, by way of being decently gracious.

"Good enough," he agreed. "To-morrow, Gray, we'll fish. It's open season for everything now and the limits are generous. Except muskellonge. You may bag only one per day of those. But trout, all kinds, bass, all kinds, pickerel, rock sturgeon—oh, we'll have the biggest time!"

"Sounds good to me," I returned, heartily. "I'm happy to be here, old scout, and we'll fish and all that, but don't put yourself about to entertain me."

"I sha'n't; but you must fall in with Lora's plans, won't you? I mean, seem pleased to attend her kettledrums and whatnot, even if it bores you."

"Of course I will. Your lady's word is law. She's a brick, isn't she?"

"Yes," and Moore smiled happily at my somewhat crude compliment. "She's just that. And such a help in my work."

"Your detective work?"

"What else? She's more than a Watson, she's a real helpmate. Her insight and intuition are marvellous, and she sees through a bit of evidence and gets the very gist of it quicker than I can."

4

"Then you surely got the right one."

"I certainly did. But I hope to Heaven there'll be no cases this summer. I want a real vacation, that's why I came 'way off here, to get away from all crime calls."

"Don't crow before you're out of the woods. Crimes can happen even in Wisconsin. And to me, this whole country round looks like a perfect setting for a first-class criminal to work in."

"Hush! I'm not superstitious, but your suggestion of such a thing might bring it about. And I don't want it!"

"You think you don't," I smiled a little, "but deep in your heart you do. You can't fish all the time, and you're even now restively hankering to be back in harness."

"Shut up!" he growled. "Talk of something pleasanter. How do you like the Dallas queen?"

"Stunning, seductive, and serpentine," I summed up the lady in question.

Moore laughed outright. "I must tell Lora that," he said. "You see, she agrees with you. Now, I think the right words are stately, gracious, and charming."

"All right," I said, "you know her better than I do, She is very beautiful, I concede."

"What do you mean, concede? Are you against her?"

"How you do snap a fellow up! No, not exactly. But I wouldn't trust her as far as I could see her,—and I'm near-sighted."

"Sometimes I think I'm no detective after all," Moore said, slowly. "Now she gives me no effect of hypocrisy or insincerity."

"But she does hint those things to Lora?"

"Y—yes, in a way."

"Then Lora's more of a detective than you are. But after I see more of the siren, I may change my mind. I didn't talk with her alone at all. What about the grumpy Mr. Ames? Is he in love with the Dallas?"

"Not at all. In the first place, he wouldn't dare be, for she is engaged to Sampson Tracy, and Tracy is not one to take kindly to any poaching on his domain. Besides that, Ames is a woman hater, also a man hater, and I think, an animal hater."

"Pleasant man!"

"Yes. He's always in a fierce mood. I don't know, but I imagine he had an affair once...."

"Oh, crossed in love and it made him queer."

"Rather say, queered in love and it made him cross."

"Yes, he looks cross. Does he always?"

"Always. He and Samp Tracy are old friends, and Samp can manage him, but nobody else can."

5

"Pleasant guest for Mr. Tracy to have about."

"He doesn't mind. Pleasure Dome is usually full of guests and if any want to sulk they are at liberty to do so."

"Pleasure Dome?"

"Yes, that's the Tracy place. It's next to this, but it's some distance off. You see, Deep Lake has a most irregular boundary line. It has all sorts of coves and inlets, and there's one that juts in behind the Tracy house. It's so deep and black and so surrounded by trees that it's called the Sunless Sea."

"Why, that's from Coleridge's 'Kubla Khan,' too."

"Yes, these are the lines:

> "In Xanadu did Kubla Khan
> A stately Pleasure Dome decree;
> Where Alph, the sacred river ran
> Through caverns measureless to man
> Down to a sunless sea.

"You know it, of course, but that will refresh your memory. Well, old Tracy——"

"Is he old?"

"Oh, no, he's forty-five, but he seems older, somehow. Well, anyway, he's romantic and poetic and imaginative. And he has a fad for Coleridge. Collects editions of him and all that. So he built his enormous and gorgeous house and called it Pleasure Dome. And the deep arm of the lake, which is right beneath his own window, he calls the Sunless Sea. And it is. It's on the north side of the house, and so hemmed in with great firs and cypresses that the sun never gets a look-in."

"Must make a delightful sleeping room!"

"Oh, there's plenty of sunlight from the east and west. His rooms are in a wing, a long L, and you bet they have sunlight and all other modern improvements. The house is a palace."

"That all sounds nice for Mrs. Dallas."

"It is. And Samp is so drivellingly, so besottedly in love with her, that she will have everything her own way when she takes up the sceptre."

"Nobody else in the family? The Tracy family, I mean."

"No. Not now. There was. You see, Tracy's sister, Mrs. Remsen, and her daughter used to live with him. Then Mrs. Remsen died, about a year ago, or a little more, and then Mrs. Dallas came into the picture, and some think it was at her request Tracy put his niece out——"

"The brute!"

6

"Oh, come now, you don't know anything about it. Alma is a lovely girl, but she's a high-handed sort—all the Tracys are—and her uncle gave her a beautiful home on a near-by island——"

"On an island? A girl, alone!"

"She has with her an old family nurse, who took care of her as a baby, and old nurse's husband is her gardener and houseman, and old nurse's daughter is her waitress, and oh, Lord, Alma Remsen is fixed all right."

"But on an island!"

"But she likes being on an island. It was her own choice. She didn't want to stay with the new wife any more than the new wife wanted to have her. You always fly off half-cocked!"

"All right, all right," I soothed him. "Tell me more."

"Well, that's all about Alma. She's a general favourite, has lots of friends, and all that, but of course, when the new mistress of Pleasure Dome comes in at the door, Alma's prospects will fly out of the window."

"Cut off entirely?"

"I'm not sure, but I've heard so. I suppose her uncle will always take care of her, but she will no longer be the Tracy heiress."

"And how does Miss Alma take that?"

"Not so good. She has had several talks with the family lawyer, and she has tried to wheedle her uncle, but he's a queer dick, is Samp Tracy, and he obstinately refuses to make a new will or even consider its terms until after he's married."

"And his present will?"

"Leaves everything to Alma. She's his only living relative. But his marriage will automatically cancel that will, and his wife will be sole inheritor unless he fixes the matter up."

"Which he will doubtless do."

"Oh, I hope so. I hope the new wife will see to it that he does. But there's where Lora has her doubts. She doesn't like Katherine Dallas, somehow."

"Lora is of great perspicacity," I said. "Where does Ames come in?"

"Regarding the fortune? Nowhere, that I know of. He is an old friend of Tracy's, both socially and in a business way. They're as different as day and night. Ames is surly, sulky, and blunt. Tracy is suave, gentle, and of the pleasantest manners."

"Miss Remsen's parents both dead?"

"Oh, yes. Her father died about fifteen years ago. Her mother recently. Had her mother lived, I suppose Tracy would have put them both out of the house, just the same. But Mrs. Remsen being gone, he sent Alma and the servants to the island house."

7

"Then the girl is utterly alone in the world except for the suave uncle and her faithful servants."

"Just that. There was a sister. Alma had a twin. But she died as a baby, or as a small child. Her little grave is in a small God's Acre on the Pleasure Dome grounds. The mother and father are buried there too. And some other relatives."

"I didn't know they had homestead cemeteries in Wisconsin. I thought they were confined to the New England states."

"It isn't usual, I believe. But the Tracys are New England stock, and, anyway, the graves are there. And beautifully kept and tended, as everything about the place has to be."

"Sounds interesting. Shall I see the high-strung Alma?"

"I didn't say high-strung. She is a normal, lovely nature. But I did say high-handed, for she is a determined sort, and if she sets her mind to a thing it has to go through."

"She has admirers?"

"Oh, of course. But she rather flouts them. One of Tracy's secretaries is frightfully in love with her. But she scarcely notices him."

"Our friend has a multiplicity of secretaries, then?"

"Two, that's all. But Sampson Tracy is a man of large interests, and I fancy he keeps the two busy. Billy Dean is the one in love with Alma, but the other, Charles Everett, is his superior."

"He's the chap who, they tell me, craves the Dallas lady."

"Yes, though of course Tracy doesn't know it. Everett wouldn't be there if he did."

"And Mrs. Dallas? What is her attitude toward the presumptuous secretary?"

"Hard to say. I think she favours him, but she is too good a financier to throw over her millionaire for his underling."

"Well, I think I've had about all the local history I can stand for one night. Let's go in the house."

To my surprise, Lora Moore and Mrs. Merrill were in the lounge, waiting for us.

The house was admirably arranged. The great central room, with doors back and front, was called the lounge, and served as both hall and living room. Off this were two smaller rooms: the card room and the music room. To one side of these rooms were the bedrooms, and on the other side, the dining room and kitchen quarters.

The furnishings were simple and attractive, with no "Mission" pieces or attempts at camping effects.

I sat down on a wide davenport beside Lora, and said, tentatively:

"I believe you and I agree in our estimate of the Dallas beauty."

"Then you have real good sense," exclaimed Lora, heartily. "Kee won't see her as I do."

"I won't either," put in Maud Merrill. "It's disgraceful to knock a woman just because she's going to marry a rich man. Rich men want wives as well as poor men. I'm all for Katherine Dallas. You're jealous, Lora, because she is so beautiful."

Lora only smiled at this, and said:

"I've really nothing against her, except that I believe she had Alma turned out of her uncle's house."

"And why not?" demanded Maud Merrill. "No house is big enough for two families; and though I don't know Miss Remsen well at all, I do know that she is a girl of strong will and decided opinions. They'd never be happy if Alma stayed there."

"I can't say as to all that," I put in, determined to have my word, "but I think, with Lora, that the Dallas is a lady of deep finesse and Machiavellian cleverness."

"Yes, just that!" cried Keeley Moore's wife.

"Well, then," said Maud, "if she snared that millionaire by her cleverness, she deserves her reward. And she deserves a peaceful home, which I doubt she'd have with a young girl bossing around, too."

"Oh, you women!" and Moore wrung his hands in mock despair, "you're making up all this. You don't know a thing about it, really."

"We can see," said Lora, sagely. "And there's no use prolonging this futile discussion. Time will show you how right I am, and meantime, we'd better all go to bed."

CHAPTER II

THE GIRL IN THE CANOE

My room at Variable Winds was cheery and comfortable. Bright-hued curtains, painted furniture and bowls full of exquisitely tinted California poppies gave the place a colourful effect that pleased my aesthetic tastes. A perfectly appointed bathroom added to my content and I concluded I would stay with the Moores as long as I could keep my welcome in good working order.

Keeley Moore was one of the best if not the best known detectives of the day, and while a quiet vacation would do him good, I was certain he was already itching to get back to his problems and mysteries, with which the city always supplied him.

I threw off my coat and put on a dressing gown, for the lake breezes were chill, and sat at a window for a final smoke.

I felt at peace with the world. Some houses give you that feeling, just as some others make you unreasonably nervous and irritable.

The moon had risen, a three-quarter or nearly full moon, and its shimmering light across the lake made me turn off my room lights and gaze out at the scene before me.

My room looked out on the lake, and the house itself was not more than a dozen yards from the water. The ground sloped gently down to a tiny bit of beach, a little crescent that had been selected for the site of the house. On the right of this placid little piece of shore was the boathouse, a large one, with canoes, rowboats and motor boats. Under the same roof was the bath house, and in front of that, out in the lake, were springboards, diving ladders and all the contrivances on which the bathers like to disport themselves.

To the left was a bit of wild, rocky shore, for the edge of the lake was greatly diversified and rocks abounded, both in and out of the water.

A line of light came across the lake, but was now and then blotted out as the swiftly drifting clouds obscured the moon.

I liked it better in the darkness, for the sight was impressive.

From my window I could see a great stretch of water, and as a background, dense black growth of trees, which came in many places down to the water's edge.

Often these trees were on a slope and rose to a height almost to be called a hill, while again the ground stretched on a low-lying level.

As I looked, the details of the landscape became clearer and I discerned a few faint lights here and there in the houses.

The big house nearest us I took to be Pleasure Dome. Not only because it was the next house, but because I could dimly distinguish a large building surmounted by a gilded dome.

How could any man in his sober senses construct such a place to live in?

It seemed like a cross between the Boston State House and the Taj Mahal.

I was really anxious to go over there and see the thing at closer range. I decided to ask Moore to take me over the next day.

Suddenly the lights all went out and the house and its dome disappeared from view. Looking at my watch I saw it was just one o'clock and concluded that the master of the house had his home darkened at that hour.

But after I again accustomed my eyes to the darkness I could see the outlines of Pleasure Dome, and it looked infinitely more attractive in the half light than it had done in the brightness of its own illumination.

As a whole, though, the lake scene was depressing. It had a melancholy, dismal air that seemed to lay a damper on my spirits. It was like a cold, clammy hand resting on my forehead. I even shook my head impatiently, as if to fling it off, and then smiled at my own foolishness. But it persisted. The lake was mournful, it even seemed menacing.

With an exclamation of disgust at my own impressionableness, I sprang up from my chair, flashed on the lights and prepared for bed.

The bright, pleasant room restored my equilibrium or equanimity or whatever it was that had been jarred, and I found myself all ready for bed, in a peaceful, happy frame of mind.

I turned off the lights, and then the lake lured me back to a last glimpse of its wild, eerie beauty.

Again I flung on my robe and sat at the window. It seemed as if I couldn't leave it. The black, sinister water, the dark shores, with deep hollows here and there, the waving, soughing trees, with thick underbrush beneath them, all seemed possessed of a spirit of evil, a frightful, uncanny spirit, that made me shiver with an unreasonable apprehension, that held me in thrall.

I have no use for premonitions, I have no faith in presentiments, but I had to admit to myself then a fear, a foreboding of some intangible, ghastly horror. Then would come the moonlight, pale and sickly now, and lasting but a moment before the clouds again blotted it out.

11

Yet I liked the darkness better, for the moon cast such horrendous shadows of those black trees into the lake that it seemed to people the lake with monstrous, maleficent beings, who leered and danced like devils.

Though I knew the hobgoblins were only the waving trees, distorted in the moonlight, I was none the less weak-minded enough to see portentous spectres that made my flesh creep.

With a half laugh and a half groan at my utter imbecility, I declared to myself that I would go to bed and go to sleep.

But as I started to rise from my chair, I saw something that made me sink back again.

The moon now was behind a light, translucent cloud, that caused a faint light on the lake.

Round a jutting corner I saw a canoe come into my line of vision.

A moment's attention convinced me that it was no ghostly craft, but an ordinary canoe, propelled by a pair of human arms.

This touch of human companionship put to rout all my feelings of fear and even my forebodings of tragedy.

Normally interested now, I watched to see who might be out at that time of night, and for what purpose.

The cloud dispersed itself, and the full clear moonlight shone down on the boat and its occupant. To my surprise it was a girl, a young-appearing girl, and she was paddling softly, but with a skilled stroke that told of long practice.

Her hair seemed to be silver in the moonlight, but I realized the light was deceptive and the curly bob might be either flaxen or gold.

She wore a white sweater and a white skirt—that much I could see plainly, but I could distinguish little more. She had no hat on, and I could see white stockings and shoes as the craft passed the house.

She seemed intent on her work, and her beautiful paddling aroused my intense admiration. She did not look up at our house at all; indeed, she seemed like an enchanted princess, doomed to paddle for her life, so earnestly did she bend to her occupation. She passed the house and kept on, in the direction of Pleasure Dome.

Could she be going there? I hardly thought so, yet I watched carefully, hanging out of my window to do so.

To my surprise she did steer her little craft straight to the great house next door, and turned as if to land there.

The Tracy house was on a line with the Moore bungalow, that is, on a curving line. They were both on the same large crescent of lake shore. Pleasure Dome had a cove or inlet behind it, Moore had told me, but that was not visible from my window. The front of the

12

house was, however, and I distinctly saw the girl beach her canoe, step lightly out and then disappear among the trees in the direction of the house.

I still sat staring at the point where she had been lost to my vision. I let the picture sink into my mind. I could see her as plainly in retrospect as I had in reality. That lissome, slender figure, that graceful springy walk—but she had limped, a very little. Not as if she were really lame, but as if she had hurt her foot or strained her ankle recently.

I speculated on who she might be. Kee had told me of no young girl living in the Tracy house now, since the niece had left there.

Ah, the niece. Could this be Sampson Tracy's niece, perhaps staying at her uncle's for a visit and coming home late from a party? But she would have had an escort or chaperon or maid—somebody would have been with her.

Yet, how could I tell that? Kee had said she was high-handed, and might she not elect to go about unescorted at any hour?

I concluded it must be the niece, for who else could it be? Then I remembered that there might be other guests at Pleasure Dome besides the morose and glum-looking Ames. This, then, might be another house guest, and perhaps the young people of the Deep Lake community were in the habit of running wild in this fashion.

Anyway, the whole episode had helped to dispel the gloom engendered by the oppressive and harrowing atmosphere of the lake scene, and I felt more cheerful. And as there was no sign of the girl's returning, I concluded she had reached the house in safety and had doubtless already gone to bed.

I tarried quite a while longer, listening to the quivering, whispering sounds of the poplars, and an occasional note from a bird or from some small animal scurrying through the woods, and finally, with a smile at my own thoughts, I snapped off the lights and got into bed.

I couldn't sleep at first, and then, just as I was about to fall asleep, I heard the light plash of a paddle.

As soon as I realized what the sound was, I sprang up and hurried to the window. But I saw no boat. Whether the same girl or some one else, the boat and whoever paddled it, were out of sight, and though I heard, or imagined I heard, a faint and diminishing sound as of paddling, I could see no craft of any sort.

I strained my eyes to see if her canoe was still beached in front of Pleasure Dome, but the moon was unfriendly now, and I could not distinguish objects on the beach.

Again I began to feel that sickening dread of calamity, that nameless horror of tragedy, and I resolutely went back to bed with a determination to stay there till morning, no matter what that God-forsaken lake did next.

I carried out this plan, and when the morning broke in a riot of sunshine, singing birds, blooming flowers and a smiling lake, I forgot all the night thoughts and their burdens and gave myself over to a joyous outlook.

Breakfast was at eight-thirty and was served on an enclosed porch looking out on the lake.

"You know, you don't have to get up at this ungodly hour," Lora said, as she smiled her greeting, "but we are wideawakes here."

"Suits me perfectly," I told her. "I've no love for the feathers after the day has really begun."

Twice during our cosy breakfast I was moved to tell about the girl in the canoe, but both times I suddenly decided not to do so. I couldn't tell why, but something forbade the telling of that tale, and I concluded to defer it, at any rate.

The chat was light and trifling. Somehow it drifted round to the subject of happiness.

"My idea of happiness," Lora said, "which I know full well I shall never attain, is to do something I want to do without feeling that I ought to be doing something else."

"Heavens and earth," exploded her husband, "any one would think you a veritable slave! What are these onerous duties you have to perform that keep you from doing your ruthers?"

Lora laughed. "Oh, not all the time, but there is much to do in a house where the servants are ill-trained and incompetent——"

"And where one has guests," Maud Merrill smiled at her, and I smiled, too.

"I'm out of it," I cried. "You ought to help your friend out, Mrs. Merrill, but, being a mere man, I can't do anything to help around the house."

Lora laughed gaily, and said, "Don't take it all too seriously. I do as I please most of the time, but—well, I suppose the truth is, I'm too conscientious."

"That's it," Kee agreed. "And you know, conscience is only a form of vanity. One wants to do right, so one can pat oneself on the back, and feel a glow of holy satisfaction."

"That's so, Kee," Lora quickly agreed, "and I oughtn't to pamper my vanity. So, I won't make that blackberry shortcake you're so fond of this morning, I'll read a novel, and bear with a smile the slings and arrows of my conscience as it reproves me."

"No," Kee told her, "that's carrying your vanity scourging too far. Make the shortcake, dear girl, not so much for me, as for Norris here. I want him to see what a bird of a cook you are."

14

Lora shook her head, but I somehow felt that the shortcake would materialize, and then Kee and I went out on the lake.

We went in a small motor launch, and he proposed that I should have a survey of the lake before we began to fish.

"It's one of the most beautiful and picturesque lakes in the county," he said, and I could easily believe that, as we continually came upon more and more rugged coves and strange rock formations.

"Those are dells," Kee said, pointing to weird and wonderful rocks that disclosed caves, grottoes, chasms, natural bridges and here and there cascades and waterfalls. "Please be duly impressed, Gray, for they are really wonderful. You know Wisconsin is the oldest state of all, I mean as to its birth. Geologists say that this whole continent was an ocean, and when the first island was thrust up above the surface of the waters, it was Wisconsin itself. Then the earth kindly threw up the other states, and so, here we are."

"I thought all these lakes were glacial."

"Oh, yes, so they are. But you don't know much, do you? The glacial period came along a lot later, and as the slow-moving fields of ice plowed down through this section they scooped out the Mississippi valley, the beds of the Great Lakes and also the beds of innumerable little lakes. There are seven thousand in Wisconsin, and two thousand in Oneida County alone."

"I am duly impressed, Kee, but quite as much by the way you rattle off this information as by the knowledge itself. Where'd you get it all?"

"Out of the Automobile Book," he returned, unabashed. "Most interesting reading. Better have a shy at it some time."

"I will. Now is this Pleasure Dome we're coming to?"

"Yes. Thought you'd like to see it. It's really a wonder house, you know. We'll be invited there to dine or something, but I want you to see it now as a picture."

It was impressive, the great pile rising against the background of dark trees, and with a foreground of brilliant flower beds, fountains, and arbours.

A critic might call it too ornate, too elaborate, but he would have to admit it was beautiful.

A building of pure white marble, its lines were simple and true, its proportions vast and noble, and save for the gilded dome, all its effects were of the utmost dignity and perfection.

And the dome, to my way of thinking, was in keeping with the majesty of it all. No lesser type of architecture could have stood it, but this semi-barbaric pile proudly upheld its glittering crown with a sublime daring that justified the whole.

15

There were numerous and involved terraces, all of white marble, that disappeared and reappeared among the trees in a fascinating way. White pergolas bore masses of beautiful flowers or vines, and back of it all rose the black, wooded slopes that surrounded most of the lake.

"We'll slip around for a glimpse of the Sunless Sea," Kee said, and I almost cried out as we came upon the place.

A strange chance had made a huge pool of water, almost square, as an arm of the lake, and this, stretched behind the house, was like a midnight sea.

Dark, even in broad daytime, because of the dense woods all round it, it also looked deep and treacherous. A slight breeze was blowing but this proved enough to ruffle the waters of the Sunless Sea in a dangerous-looking way.

"Don't go in there!" I cried, and Kee turned aside.

"I didn't intend to," he said, "I was just throwing a scare into you. It's really devilish. A sudden wave can suck you down to interminable depths. You're not afraid, really?"

"Oh, no," I assured him, "but it's pesky frightensome to look at, especially——"

Again I was on the verge of telling him of the scene on the lake the night before, and again I stopped, held back by some force outside myself.

"Especially why?" he asked, curiously, but I evaded the issue by saying, "Especially when one is on a holiday."

He laughed and we turned away from Pleasure Dome.

"Now I'll show you the island," he said, "and then we'll tackle the tackle."

We went rapidly back past Pleasure Dome, on down the lake, past Moore's own place, and then on a bit farther to the Island.

"They call it 'Whistling Reeds', and it's a good name," he said. "When the wind's a certain way, and it's quiet otherwise, you can hear the reeds whistle like birds."

"You do have most interesting places," I said. "And who lives here? And where's the house?"

"Alma Remsen lives here, the niece of Sampson Tracy I told you about last night. You can't see the house, the trees are so thick."

"I should say they were!" and I stared at the dense black mass. "Why doesn't she cut a vista, at least?"

"She doesn't want it, I believe. Thinks it's more picturesque like this."

"I'd be scared to death to live there!"

"No reason to be. Nothing untoward ever happens up here. All peaceable citizens."

16

"But fancy living in such a place. How do they get provisions and all that?"

"Oh, that's easy. Lots of the dealers deliver their stuff in canoes or motor boats. See, there's the boathouse. Some day we'll call here. Alma likes my wife, she'll be glad to see us."

"I suppose she's a canoeist."

"Everybody's that, around here. I mean the people who live all the year round. A good many people live on islands. They like it. This island, you see, is a big one. About two or three acres, say. That gives Miss Remsen room for tennis courts and gardens and pretty much anything she wants, and the house is very pleasant. Nothing like Pleasure Dome, but a bigger house than the one we're in."

We turned then, and started off toward the spot where Kee elected to do his fishing.

"Hello," he said, as we moved on, "there's Alma now. That's Miss Remsen."

We were now about midway between the Moore bungalow and the Island of Whistling Reeds. I looked, to see a girl come down to the floating dock of the boathouse, spring into a canoe and paddle away.

I said nothing aloud, but to myself I said it was the girl I had seen in a canoe the night before.

There was no mistaking that slim, lithe figure, that graceful capable way of managing the boat, and she even wore what seemed to me to be the same clothes, a white skirt and white sweater. She had on a small white felt hat, and I noticed that she did not limp at all. As I had surmised, the limp was occasioned by some slight and temporary strain or bruise.

"Well, don't eat her up with your eyes!" exclaimed Moore, and I realized I had been staring.

Also I was just about to tell him of seeing her before, but the chaffing tone he used somehow shut me up on the subject.

So I only said, gaily: "Bowled over by the Lady of the Lake!" and laughed back at him.

"That's what she's called up here," he informed me. "She's in her canoe so much and manages it so perfectly, she seems like a part of it. Of course, wherever she goes, she has to go in that or in some boat. Can't get on and off an island in a motor car."

"Must be an awful nuisance."

"She doesn't find it so. Says she likes it better than a motor. Look at her paddle. Isn't she an expert?"

"She sure is." And I held my tongue tightly to refrain from saying that she seemed to me to have paddled even more beautifully the night before. But, I said to myself, that was doubtless the

17

glamour loaned by the moonlight and the witchery of the night scene.

Miss Remsen soon reached Pleasure Dome, and we could see her beach her canoe and follow her with our eyes for a few steps until she disappeared behind a clump of tall trees.

We set to work then in good earnest and I saw in Keeley Moore for the time being an embodiment of perfect happiness.

He loved to fish, even alone, but better still, he loved to fish with a congenial companion. And we were that. Though not friends of such very long standing, we were similar in our likes and dislikes as well as in our dispositions.

We had an identical liking for silence at times, and as a rule we chose the same times. Often we would sit for half an hour in a sociable silence, and then break into the most animated conversation.

This morning, after we had begun to fish, such a spell fell upon us. I was glad, for I wanted to think things out; to learn, if possible, why I was so interested, or why, indeed, I was interested at all, in Alma Remsen.

Just because I saw her paddling over to her uncle's house the night before and again this morning, was that enough to make me feel that I must keep still about the first excursion? And, if so, why?

I didn't even know yet what she looked like. So it couldn't be that I had fallen for a pretty face—I didn't even know whether she had one.

I thought of asking Kee that, but decided not to. A strange, vague instinct held me back from mentioning Alma Remsen's name.

Suddenly he said, "Damn!" in a most explosive way, and not unnaturally I thought he had lost one of those biggest of all big fishes.

But as he began pulling in his empty line and making other evident preparations for bringing our fishing party to an end, I mildly asked for light on the subject.

"Got to go home," he said, like a sulky child.

"What for?"

"See that red flag in the bungalow window? That means come home at once. Lora only uses it in cases of real importance, so we've got to go."

CHAPTER III

THE TRAGEDY

As we went up the steps and crossed the porch of the Moore bungalow, we saw a man seated in the lounge, talking to Lora.

Both jumped up at our approach, and Lora cried out, "Oh, Kee, Mr. Tracy is dead!"

"Sampson Tracy! Dead?" exclaimed Moore, with a look of blank consternation.

"Yes," the man said, tersely, "and not only dead, but murdered. I'm Police Detective March. I've just come from the Tracy house. You see, everything is at sixes and sevens over there. Nobody authorized to take the helm, though plenty of them want to do so. In a way, Everett, the secretary, is head of the heap, but a guest there, Mr. Ames, refuses to acknowledge that Everett has any say at all. Claims he is Tracy's oldest and closest friend, and insists on taking charge himself."

"Why shouldn't he?" asked Keeley Moore, quietly.

"Well, why should he?" countered the policeman. "And, besides, I think he's the man who killed Tracy. But here's my errand here. It seems Mr. Ames was here last night to dinner?"

Lora nodded assent to his inquiring glance.

"Well, he formed a high opinion of Mr. Moore's detective ability, and he wants to engage his services, if possible."

Kee Moore was a tall, dark man, about thirty-five or so. But when he undertook a case, or even thought about undertaking a case, he seemed to change his personality. Rather, he intensified it. He seemed to be taller, darker and older.

I saw this change come over him at once, as he listened to the police detective's words.

There is a phrase about an old warhorse scenting the battle. I've never seen such a thing, but I am sure it implies the same attitude that Moore showed at the moment. His eyes took on a far-away look that was yet alert and receptive. His hands showed strained muscles as he grasped the back of a chair that stood in front of him. His lips lost their smiling curve and set in a straight line. I knew all these gestures well, and I knew that not only would he take up this case, but that he was anxious to get at it at once.

Lora knew it, too, and I heard her sigh as she resigned herself to the inevitable. It wasn't necessary for any of us to say we had hoped Kee was to have a rest from his work, an idle vacation. The two

19

Moores and I knew that, and we all knew, too, that the vacation was broken in upon and there would be no rest for the busy, inquiring brain until the Tracy case was settled for all time.

"I don't know about accepting this offer of Mr. Ames to engage my services," Kee said, "but I will most certainly look into the matter and if I can be of help we can make definite arrangements. Tell me a little more of the circumstances, please, and then we will go over to Pleasure Dome."

"It seems the butler or housekeeper was in the habit of taking tea to Mr. Tracy's room of a morning, at nine o'clock. Well, this morning, the door was locked and nobody responded to knocks on it. So—you can get the connecting data later, sir—they broke in, and found Mr. Tracy dead in bed, with the strangest doings all about."

"What do you mean by strange doings?"

"Well, he was all dolled up with flowers and a long red scarf, and, if you please, a red feather duster sticking up behind his head-"

"Did you see all this?" demanded Moore, his eyes growing darker every minute.

"Yes, and that's not half! There was an orange in his hand and crackers on his pillow and a crucifix against his breast——"

"Come on," said Moore, quietly, but in a tone of suppressed excitement. "Let's get over there before they disturb all that scenery! I never heard of such astounding conditions."

"No, sir, I'll say you didn't," March agreed. "I felt a bit miffed when they told me to come and get you; any detective would, you know, but when I came to think over all that hodge-podge of evidence, I knew it was a case too big for me to tackle alone. I hope you'll let me help you, sir."

"Oh, of course," said Moore, a little impatiently, as he urged the detective to start. "Will your car hold us all?" His glance included me, and March answered; "Oh, yes. I've one of Mr. Tracy's big cars."

When we reached the great house, and stopped at the landing place under the porte-cochère, I was more than ever impressed by the beauty all about.

There was nothing glaring or ostentatious. The bit of verandah we traversed to reach the front door was brightened with a few railing flower-boxes and potted palms, but it was quietly dignified and stately.

Stately was the key word for the whole place, and I suddenly remembered that Kubla Khan's Pleasure Dome was described as stately. Surely, Sampson Tracy had sensed the real meaning of the phrase.

Inside, the house was the same. Marked everywhere by good taste, the appointments were of the finest and best.

20

There seemed to be a great many people about. Servants were coming and going and policemen were here and there.

March took Moore and myself directly to the library, where Inspector Farrell was awaiting us.

Also present were Ames, whom we already knew, and a young man, who proved to be Charles Everett, the confidential secretary of the dead man.

I took to Everett at once. He was the clean-cut type of so many of our efficient young American secretaries. He looked capable and wise, and being introduced, bowed gravely.

Ames took up the matter at once.

He looked perturbed rather than grumpy this morning, but his speaking voice had an unpleasant twang, and I saw Kee stiffen up as if he would certainly decline to be at this man's beck and call.

"I sent for you, Mr. Moore," Ames began, "to get your help in unravelling the mystery of Sampson Tracy's death. As you will soon learn, the conditions are startlingly unusual, even bizarre. But I have heard that the more bizarre the clues and evidence, the easier a case is to solve. So, I beg you to get at it at once and exert your most clever efforts."

"But I haven't yet said I would take the case for you," Moore told him.

"Why not?" cried Ames, his face lowering in a pettish frown. "I shall make no objection to your terms, whatever they may be—in reason. I shall not trammel you with any restrictions or annoy you with any advice. I am told you are a famous detective. I know you for a friend of Mr. Tracy. Why, then, would you hesitate to solve the problem of his death and learn the identity of his murderer?"

"Are you sure he was murdered?" asked Moore. "You see, I know little of the facts in the case."

"No," broke in Inspector Farrell, "no, we don't know that he was murdered. And the facts that we do know are seemingly contradictory. I trust, Mr. Moore, that you will look into the matter, at least, and give us the benefit of your findings, whether you officially take up the case or not."

"I cannot say," Moore told him, "until I am in possession of the details of the tragedy. Nor do I want it told me here. Let me see the body, let me inquire for myself concerning the facts, and let me draw my own conclusions. Only after that can I decide whether I take on the case or not."

"I think you very unreasonable, Mr. Moore," Ames grumbled. "I want you to be my agent in this matter, and so I want you to start in fully equipped with my sanction and authority."

21

"Just how much authority have you here, Mr. Ames?" asked Moore, looking at him thoughtfully.

"As the oldest and nearest friend of Sampson Tracy, and as his intimate confidant and adviser, I think I can claim more authority than any one else. In fact the man had no relatives in the world except a niece. He had no friends of a confidential nature except myself. I am not referring to financial affairs, they are in the hands of his lawyer and his secretaries. But if he has been murdered, I propose to hound down the wretch who is responsible for his death. I know much about Tracy's life that nobody else knows. I know of those who might wish him dead, and my knowledge, combined with the skill of a canny detective, must bring out the truth."

This was straightforward talk, and Ames, though his face wore an aggrieved expression, spoke concisely and to the point. But after all, his manner was truculent, he didn't ask Moore's help so much as he demanded it, almost commandeered it. I was not surprised to see Kee stick to his first decision.

"I appreciate all you say, Mr. Ames," Kee said, "but I repeat I am not willing to take a case until I look into it. Do not delay further, but let us go at once to the scene of the tragedy."

Ames glowered, but without another word he led the way from the room and turned toward the staircase.

The broad steps, carpeted with red velvet, branched half way up, and turning to the right, Ames conducted us to Sampson Tracy's rooms. They were in a wing that had been flung out at the back of the house, probably as a later addition to the structure. Entrance was through a private hall, and then into a foyer or ante-room, from which led several doors.

"This is the bedroom," said the Inspector, taking a key from his pocket as he paused before one of the doors.

"I thought you had to break in," Moore said, looking at the unmarred door.

"Not exactly," Farrell told him. "The door was locked and the key inside, in the lock. But they got the garage mechanician up here, and he managed to dislodge the key and then get the door unlocked with his tools."

He opened the door, and we filed in, the Inspector first, then Moore and I, then Ames and Detective March.

Farrell closed and locked the door behind us, and it was then that I saw the strange, the grotesque spectacle of Sampson Tracy's deathbed.

The first thing that caught my attention and from which I found it well nigh impossible to detach my vision was the red-feather duster.

A full plume of bright red feathers seemed to crown the head on the pillow.

The handle of the duster had been thrust down behind and under the head, and only the red plume showed, of such fine, light feathers that a few fronds waved at a step across the room or a movement near the bed.

Then I looked at the rest of the strange picture.

Sampson Tracy was a large and heavy man. His head was large, and his face was of the conformation sometimes called pear-shaped. He had heavy jaws, pendulous jowls and a large mouth. Clean shaven as to face, his hair was thick and rather long. His eyebrows were bushy, and his half opened eyes of a glassy and yet dull blue.

His hair was iron-gray, and round his brow were wreathed some blossoms of blue larkspur. Across his chest, diagonally, was a garland of the same flowers. The blossoms were not tied or twined, they had merely been laid in a row in order to form a vinelike garland.

The right hand, bent to rest on his breast, held a crucifix, and in the left hand was, of all things, a small orange.

His head lay on one large pillow, and on the other pillow was a folded handkerchief and also two small sweet crackers. And encircling the head and shoulders, framing all these strange details, a long and wide scarf, of soft and filmy scarlet chiffon, a beautiful scarf, from a woman's point of view, but a peculiar adjunct to a man's taking-off.

I stared at all this, quite forgetting to look at Moore to see how he was taking it.

When I did glance up at him, hearing his voice, I saw he had evidently completed his scrutiny of the bed and had turned to Harper Ames.

"Why do you think Mr. Tracy was murdered?" Kee asked of the glum-faced one.

"What other theory is possible?" Ames returned. "A suicide would not place all that flumadiddle about himself. A natural death wouldn't have such decorations, either. So, he was killed, either by some one with a most distorted sense of humour, or there is a meaning in each seeming bit of foolishness."

"What did he die of, exactly?"

"That we don't know yet, the doctor will be here any minute, and the coroner, too."

Even as he spoke, Doctor Rogers arrived. He was the family physician, and as Farrell opened the door to his knock, he went straight to the bed.

"What's all this rubbish?" he exclaimed, reaching for the scarf.

23

"Don't touch it, If you can help it, Doctor," March implored him. "It may be evidence——"

"Evidence of what?"

"Crime—murder—or is it a natural death?"

Doctor Rogers was making his examination with as little disturbance as might be of the flowers and scarf.

But the feather duster he pulled from its place and flung across the room. The orange followed it, and the crackers.

"Pick them up if you want them for clues," he said; "you know where they were found, and I won't have my friend photographed with all those monkey tricks about him!"

March picked up the things, with a due regard for possible finger prints, and stored them away in a drawer of the chiffonier.

Finally, Doctor Rogers straightened up from his examining, and rose to his feet.

"Apoplexy," he said. "What's all this talk about murder? Sampson Tracy is dead of apoplexy, as I have often told him he would be, if he kept on with his plan of eating and drinking too much and taking little or no exercise. He had an apoplectic stroke last night which proved fatal. He died, as nearly as I can judge, about two o'clock. As to these foolish trinkets, they were brought in here later and placed round him after he was dead. You can see that though he seemed to hold the cross and the orange in his hands, they weren't tightly held, the fingers were bent round them after death. It must have been the deed of some child or of some servant who is mentally lacking. Is there a girl of twelve or fourteen on the place? But I've no time to tarry now. I'm on my way to the train. I'm going for my vacation on a trip through Canada and down the Pacific coast. I'd throw it over, of course, if I could be of any use. But I can't, and my wife is waiting for me. I've given my statement as to Tracy's death, and I know I'm right. Here comes Coroner Hart now. I say, Hart, the Inspector and Mr. Ames here will tell you my findings, and I know you'll corroborate me. It's all a terrible pity, but I knew he was digging his grave with his teeth. No amount of advice did a bit of good. As to the flowers and rags, look for a twelve-year-old girl.... There are the ones who kick up such bobberies. Maybe the housekeeper has a grandchild, or maybe there is a kiddy in the chauffeur's or gardener's cottage. Good-bye, I must run. Sorry, but to lose this local train means to upset our reservations all along the trip."

The Doctor hurried away, yet so positive had been his diagnosis, and so logical his disinclination to linger when he could be of no possible use, that we all forgave him in our minds.

The Coroner gave a start at the masses of flowers, somewhat

24

disarranged by Doctor Rogers's manipulations, and drew nearer to the body.

Farrell told him how things had been before Doctor Rogers removed the feather duster and threw out the orange and crackers.

"He ought to have let them alone!" Hart declared, angrily.

"It doesn't really matter," put in March, "I know exactly how they were lying, and anyway, Rogers says it's a natural death."

"Natural? With all that gimcrack show!"

"He says that's the work of a mischievous child, for preference, a little girl of twelve or fourteen."

"He's thinking of Poltergeist—he's got that sort of thing on the brain. Let me take a look at the body."

So Doctor Hart sat on the side of the bed and made his examination of the dead millionaire.

"There is every symptom of apoplexy," he said, at last, "and no symptom of anything else. Yet, I feel a little uncertainty. We'll have to see what the autopsy says."

"When can you have that?" Ames asked him.

"Very soon. This afternoon, probably. But it is important now to make inquiries as to conditions last night. You were here, Mr. Ames?"

"Yes,—that is, I am staying here, visiting, you know,—but last evening I was out to dinner, with our neighbour, Mr. Moore here."

"What time did you get home?"

"Not late; about eleven, I think."

"Had Mr. Tracy gone to bed then?"

"No, he was waiting up for me. We went into the smoking room and had a smoke and a chat."

"What time did you retire?"

"We went upstairs about midnight, I should say. I said good night to him on this floor and then went on upstairs to my own room."

"He seemed in his usual health and spirits?"

"So far as I noticed, yes."

"You heard nothing unusual in the night?"

"Nothing at all."

"What was the subject of your conversation last evening?"

"Nothing of serious moment. He asked me who were at the Moore party and I told him. He was lightly interested, but cared only to hear about Mrs. Dallas, who is his fiancée and who was at the party."

"And Mr. Tracy was not there?"

"No. He had been invited, but—well, he had had a little tiff with the lady, and in a moment of anger had declined the invitation. He

25

was sorry afterward and wished he had accepted it. I begged him to go in my place, I would have willingly stayed home, but he wouldn't hear of such a thing. Then I wanted to telephone Mrs. Moore, the hostess, and ask her to make room for him, too, but he wouldn't allow that, either. So I went to the dinner, and Mrs. Dallas went, but Mr. Tracy stayed at home."

"Alone?"

"I think so, except for his two secretaries. When I came home, he was in a pleasant enough mood, and I concluded he had thought it all over and straightened it out in his mind one way or another. I didn't refer to the matter at all, but he asked me many questions about Mrs. Dallas, such as how she looked, what mood she was in and whether she said anything about him. Just such questions as a man would naturally ask about his absent sweetheart."

"All this properly belongs to the inquest," Coroner Hart said. "But I want to get any side-lights I can while the matter is fresh in your mind. Do you know this room well, Mr. Ames?"

"Not at all. I've only been in here once or twice in my life."

"Then you can't tell me if anything is missing?"

"No, I think not," Ames looked around. "No, I don't know anything about the appointments here. Or do you mean valuables?"

"Anything at all. I think we can't blink the fact that somebody came in here after the man was dead, and arranged all those weird decorations. Now maybe that somebody took away something as well."

"That I don't know," Ames reiterated. "I know nothing of Tracy's belongings."

The man had been pleasant enough at first, but now he was resuming his irritable manner, and I wondered if he would get really angry.

Keeley Moore was saying almost nothing. But I knew he was losing no points of what was happening, and I rather expected him to break out soon. He did.

"Perhaps, Doctor Hart," he said, quietly, "it might be a good idea to get Mr. Tracy's manservant or housekeeper up here, and find out a little more about the appointments of this room. For instance, whether the orange and crackers were already here, or whether the mysterious visitor brought them."

"I was just about to do that, Mr. Moore," the Coroner said, with such haste that I had my doubts of his veracity.

But he rang a bell in the wall, and we waited for a response.

The butler himself answered it, a rather grandiose personage in the throes of excitement and grief at the terrible happenings to his master.

"Well, Griscom," Ames said, with his habitual frown, "these gentlemen want to ask you some questions. Answer them as fully as you can."

"Was it Mr. Tracy's habit to have a bit of fruit or a cracker in his room at night?" the Coroner inquired.

"Yes, sir," said the butler, and the sound of his own voice seemed to steady him. "He always had an orange or a few grapes and a cracker or two on the table by his bed, sir."

"And do you think this orange and these crackers are the ones put out for him last night?"

"I'm sure of it, sir. I put them out myself."

"Then where is the plate? Surely you had them on a plate."

"Of course, sir. They were on a small gilt-edged plate. I don't see it about."

"No, I don't either. Had Mr. Tracy a valet?"

"No, sir, he didn't like a man fussing about. I attended him, sir, and a footman helped me out now and then; and Mrs. Fenn, she's cook and housekeeper, sir, she looked after his clothes, saving what I did myself."

"Have you any reason to think your master would take his own life?"

"Oh, Lord, no, sir. Begging your pardon, but he was very fond of life, was Mr. Tracy. I thought he died of a fit, sir."

"Probably he did. A fit or stroke of apoplexy. I begin to think, Inspector, we have no murder mystery on our hands after all."

"No," said Farrell, shaking his head, "apparently not."

"Apparently yes," said Keeley Moore, quietly. He had been looking at the dead man, and though he had not moved, but had stood for a long time, with his hands in his pockets, staring down at the still figure on the bed, I knew, somehow, that he had made a discovery.

"Stand over here, please, Inspector," he said, in his calm, matter-of-fact way.

Farrell went and stood beside him, and Moore pointed to a very small circular object that shone like silver, though nearly hidden by the thick and rather long hair of Sampson Tracy.

It was the head of a nail that had been driven into the man's skull.

CHAPTER IV

THE NAIL

"My God!" Farrell exclaimed, stepping closer and pushing aside the gray hair, thus clearly revealing the awful truth.

A flat-headed nail, the head rather more than a quarter of an inch in diameter, had been driven into the skull with such force that it showed merely as a metal disk. Having been hidden by the dead man's hair, it had remained unnoticed until Moore's quick eyes espied it.

Farrell picked at it a little, but it was far too firmly fastened to be moved by his fingers.

"What shall we do?" the Inspector asked, helplessly. "Shall we try to get Doctor Rogers back?"

"No," returned the Coroner, "he's just starting on a long trip. Let him go. He could do nothing and it would be a pity to spoil his journey. His diagnosis of apoplexy was most natural in the circumstances, for the symptoms are the same. I, too, thought death was the result of an apoplectic stroke. But now we know it is black murder, the case comes directly within my jurisdiction, and there's no occasion to recall Doctor Rogers."

"You're right," Ames assented, "but who could have done this fearful thing? I can hardly believe a human being capable of such a horror! Mr. Moore, you simply must take up this case. It ought to be a problem after your own heart."

Every word the man uttered made me dislike him more. To refer to this terrible tragedy as a problem after Moore's own heart seemed to me to indicate a mind callous and almost ghoulish in its type.

I knew Kee well enough to feel sure that he would investigate the murder, but not at the behest of Harper Ames.

He only acknowledged Ames's speech by a noncommittal nod and turned to Detective March.

"We have our work cut out for us," he said, very gravely. "I have never seen a stranger case. The murderer must have been a man of brute passions and brute strength. That nail is almost imbedded in the bone, and, I fancy, needed more than one blow of the hammer that drove it in. But first, as to the doors and windows. You tell me they were locked this morning?"

"Yes, sir," answered Griscom, the butler, as Moore looked at him.

He was a smallish man, bald and with what are sometimes called pop-eyes. He stared in a frightened manner, but he controlled his voice as he went on to tell his story.

"Yes, sir, I brought the master's tea at nine o'clock, as always. The door was locked——"

"Is it usually locked in the morning?" Moore interrupted.

"Sometimes, not always. When it is locked, I knock and Mr. Tracy would get up and open the door. If unlocked, I walked right in."

"And this morning it was locked, and the key in the lock on the inside?"

"Yes, sir. So I knocked, but when there was no answer, I got scared——"

"Why were you scared?"

"Because Doctor Rogers had often told me that Mr. Tracy was in danger of an apoplectic stroke, and that I must do anything I could to make him eat less and take more exercise. I've been with the master a long time, sir, and I had the privilege of a bit of talk with him now and then. So I did try to persuade him to obey the doctor's orders, and he would laugh and promise to do so. But he forgot it as soon as he saw some dish he was fond of, and he'd eat his fill of it."

"Go on, Griscom," Moore said, "what happened next?"

"I went to Mr. Everett——"

"Yes, he went to Everett," broke in the aggrieved voice of Harper Ames. "Why did he do that, instead of coming to me, I'd like to know!"

"Go on," Moore instructed the butler.

"I went to Mr. Everett, sir, he was up and dressed, and he said, at once, to get Louis—that's the chauffeur—and tell him to bring some tools, I did that, and Louis first pushed the key out of the lock, and then poked around with a wire until he got the door open. Then we came in——"

"Who came in?"

"Mr. Everett and Mr. Ames and me, sir. And Mrs. Fenn—she's the housekeeper—she saw Louis running upstairs, so she came, too."

"And you saw——?"

"Mr. Tracy, just as he was when you first saw him, sir. Just as he is now, except for the things Doctor Rogers chucked out."

"Is that door, the one that was locked, the entrance to the whole suite?"

"Yes, sir, that door is the only one connecting these rooms with the house."

"I see. Now what about the windows?"

"They haven't been touched, sir."

Kee Moore turned his attention to the windows. There were many of them. The suite of Sampson Tracy's was a rectangular wing, built out from the main house, and having windows on three sides. But all of these windows overlooked the deep, black waters of the Sunless Sea. It had been the whim of the man to have his quarters thus, to be surrounded on all sides by the water of the lake that he loved, and he usually had all the windows wide open, doubtless enjoying the lake breezes that played through the rooms, and listening to the birds, whose notes broke the stillness of the night.

"What is below these rooms?" Moore asked.

"The big ballroom, sir. Nothing else."

After scrutinizing every window in the bedroom, dressing room, bathroom and sitting room, Moore said, slowly: "These windows seem to me to be inaccessible from below."

It was characteristic of the man that he didn't say they were inaccessible but merely that they seemed so to him.

As they certainly did to the rest of us. We all looked out, and in every instance, the sheer drop to the lake was about fifteen or more feet. The outer walls of marble presented no foothold for even the most daring of climbers. They were smooth, plain, and absolutely unscalable.

"It is certain no one entered by the windows," Moore said, at last, having looked out of every one. "I suppose the house is always carefully secured at night?"

"Yes, sir," Griscom assured him. "Mr. Tracy was very particular about that. He and all the household had latchkeys, and the front door—indeed, all the doors and windows were carefully seen to."

"Who has latchkeys?"

"Mr. Everett, Mr. Dean, myself and the housekeeper. Then there are others which are given to guests. Mr. Ames had one——"

"With so many latchkeys about, one may have been abstracted by some evil-minded person."

"Not likely, sir. We keep strict watch on them."

"Well, that would only give entrance to the house. How could anyone get into and out of Mr. Tracy's room, leaving the door locked on the inside?"

I knew Moore purposely voiced this problem himself, to head off those who would ask it of him. He had often said to me, "if you don't want a question asked of you, ask it yourself of somebody else." And so, as he flung this at them each felt derelict in not being able to reply.

But Ames's querulous voice volleyed the question back.

"That's why I want you to do up this business, Moore," he said. "That's what makes it such a pretty problem——"

Moore could stand this no longer.

"For an intimate friend of a martyred man, I should think you would see the matter in a more personal light than a pretty problem!"

"Oh, I do. I'm sad and sorry enough, but I don't wear my heart on my sleeve. And first of all, I'm keen to avenge my friend. And I know that what's to be done must be done quickly. So, get busy, I beg."

The more Ames said, the less I liked him, and I knew Kee felt the same way about it. But the man was right as to haste being advisable. The circumstances were so peculiar, the conditions so fantastic, that search for the criminal must be made quickly, or a man of such diabolical cleverness would put himself beyond our reach.

The Inspector, the police detective and Keeley Moore consulted a few moments and then Inspector Farrell said:

"The case is altered. Now that we know it is wilful murder, and not a stroke of illness, we must act accordingly. Coroner Hart will conduct an immediate inquiry, preliminary to his formal inquest. No one may leave the house; you, Griscom, will tell the servants this, and I shall call in more help from the police station to guard the place. We will go downstairs, and the Coroner will choose a suitable room, and begin his investigation."

Farrell was an efficient director, though in no way a detective. He locked the door that commanded the whole apartment after he had herded us all out.

We filed downstairs, and I could hear women's voices in a small reception room as we passed it.

The Coroner chose a room which was fitted up as a sort of writing room. It was of moderate size and contained several desks or writing tables, evidently a writing room for guests. There was a bookcase of books and a table of periodicals and newspapers.

Clearly, the house had every provision for comfort and pleasure. Save for the sinister atmosphere now pervading it, I felt I should have liked to visit there.

The Coroner settled himself at a table, and instructed Griscom to send in the house servants one at a time. He also told the butler to serve breakfast as usual, and advised Harper Ames to go to the dining room, as he would be called on later for testimony.

Hart's manner now was crisp and business-like. The realization of the awful facts of the case had spurred him to definite and immediate action.

31

Mrs. Fenn, the cook-housekeeper, threw no new light on the situation. She corroborated Griscom's story of the locked door and the subsequent opening of it by Louis, but she could add no new information.

"You were fond of Mr. Tracy?" asked Moore, kindly, for the poor woman was vainly trying to control her grief.

"Oh, yes, sir. He was a good master and a truly great man."

"You've never known, among the guests of the house, any one who was his enemy?"

"No, sir. But I almost never see the guests. I'm housekeeper, to be sure, but the maids do all the housework. I superintend the cooking."

"And you've heard no gossip about any one who had an enmity or a grudge toward Mr. Tracy?"

"Ah, who could have? He was a gentle, peaceable man, was Mr. Tracy. Who could wish him harm?"

"Yet somebody did," the Coroner put in, and then he dismissed Mrs. Fenn, feeling she could be of no use.

The other house servants were similarly ignorant of any guest or neighbour who was unfriendly to Mr. Tracy, and then Hart called for the chauffeur.

Louis, a Frenchman, was different in manner and disinclined to talk. In fact, he refused to do so unless all members of the household were sent from the room.

So the Coroner ordered everybody out except Farrell and Detective March, Moore and myself.

Then Louis waxed confidential and declared that Mr. Ames and Mr. Tracy were deadly enemies.

I thought the man was exaggerating, and that he had some grudge of his own against Ames. But Hart listened avidly to the chauffeur's arraignment, and I was forced to the conclusion that Louis knew a lot.

Yet it was all hints and innuendoes. He stated that the two men were continually quarrelling. Asked what about, he replied "Money matters."

"What sort of money matters?" Hart asked him.

"Stocks and bonds and mortgages. I think Mr. Ames owed Mr. Tracy a great deal of money and he couldn't or wouldn't pay it, and so they wrangled over it."

"There was no quarrelling on other subjects?"

"No, sir, except now and then about Mrs. Dallas."

"And what about her?"

"Well, Mr. Ames didn't want Mr. Tracy to marry her."

"Did Mr. Ames favour the lady himself?"

"Oh, no, sir. He's a woman hater. Or at least he says so. No, but he didn't want Mr. Tracy to marry anybody for fear he might cut him, Mr. Ames, out of his will."

"How do you know all these things?"

"Well, I drive the car, you see, and they talk these matters over, and I can't help hearing them. They make no bones of it, they talk right out. I never repeat anything I hear, in an ordinary way, but as you ask me, sir——"

"Yes, Louis, tell all you know. So Mr. Ames would suffer financially if Mr. Tracy married?"

"I don't know that, sir, but I know he thought he would. And I suppose he knew."

"It seems to me," Farrell said, "we ought to know the terms of Mr. Tracy's will as it might help us to get at the truth."

"We can't do that at the moment," Hart said, "and anyway, this is merely a preliminary inquiry to get the main facts of the situation."

But the other servants had no more information to impart than those hitherto questioned. A chambermaid, one Sally Bray, convinced us that all the queer decorations spread on the bed had been already in the room and were, therefore, not brought in by the murderer.

The red feather duster belonged in a small cupboard that held polishing cloths and dusters. The larkspur flowers had been in a vase on a side table, and the whole bunch had been removed from the vase and laid around the dead man. The orange and crackers had been on a plate on the bedside table, but where the plate was, Sally had no idea. The crucifix was Mr. Tracy's property and belonged on a small hook above the head of his bed.

"And the scarf," suggested Hart. "The red chiffon scarf, where did that come from?"

Sally blushed and looked down, but finally being urged to tell, said that she knew it to be a scarf belonging to Mrs. Dallas, and the lady had left it there one evening not long ago, when she had been there to dinner.

"Why had it not been returned to her?" Hart wanted to know.

"Because Mr. Tracy took a notion to it. It was a sort of keepsake of the lady, sir, and, too, Mr. Tracy was that fond of beautiful things. Any pretty piece of silk or brocade would please him tremenjous."

"Then, whoever arranged all those decorations round him knew of his love for beautiful things, and that would explain the flowers and the scarf. Is there anything missing from his room, Sally?"

"I don't know, sir. I've not been allowed in there this morning."

"Well, go up there now. Tell the guard he's to let you in. Here's the key."

"Oh, sir, I—I daren't! Don't make me go in there!"

The girl shivered with real fear, but Hart had to know.

"You must go," he said, not unkindly. "Get Griscom to go with you, or Mrs. Fenn, if you like. But it is important for me to know if anything has been taken away that you know of. I don't mean papers or letters from his desk. I mean any of his appointments or small belongings."

The girl went off, still shuddering, and Hart finished up the rest of the servants in short order.

Next he interviewed Charlie Everett. I had taken a fancy to Everett, and somehow, from the way Kee looked at him, I thought he liked him, too.

He was not a distinguished-looking man, but he seemed a well-balanced sort, and his eyes were alert and showed a sense of humour. Not that the occasion called for humour, but you can always tell by a man's eyes if he has that desirable trait.

Very quiet and self-possessed was Everett, his manner polite but a little detached. He was quite ready to answer questions but he gave only the answer, no additional information.

Yes, he said, he had spent an hour or so with Mr. Tracy the night before. They had played a game of billiards and had then sat for a short time over a cigar and a whisky and soda. Then, perhaps about ten o'clock, he had said good night to his employer and had gone to his own room. No, he could form no idea whatever as to who could have killed Sampson Tracy, or how he could have got into the room.

"That is," he amended his speech, "he could get in easy enough, but I don't see how he could get out and leave the door locked behind him."

"It is one of those cases," Hart said, a little sententiously, "where there has been a murder committed in a sealed room."

Keeley Moore spoke up then.

"A murder cannot be committed in a sealed room," he said, "unless the murderer stays there. If the murderer left the room, the room was not a sealed room."

"How did he get out?" demanded Hart.

"That we have yet to learn. But he did get out, not through the door to the hall. Remains the possibility of a secret passage and the windows."

"I'm sure there is no secret passage," Everett said, with an unusual burst of unasked information. "I've been here three years and if there was such a thing I'm sure I'd know of it."

34

"You might and you might not," said Moore, looking at him. "If Mr. Tracy wanted a private entrance to his suite for any reason, he would have had it built and kept the matter quiet."

"Not Sampson Tracy," exclaimed Everett. "He was not a secretive man. I think I may say I knew all about his affairs, both business matters and private dealings, and he trusted me absolutely."

"Even so," Moore told him. "But in the lives of most men there is some secret, something that they don't talk over with anybody."

"Not Mr. Tracy," Everett reiterated. "Even his engagement to Mrs. Dallas was freely talked over with me, both before it occurred and since. I know all about his habits and his fads and whims. And in no case was there ever an occasion for a secret passage to or from his rooms."

"Yet it may be there," Kee insisted. "But if none can be found, then the murderer either escaped by the windows or——"

"Or what?" asked Hart.

"Or he had a steel wire contraption to turn the key from the outside. But this I don't think likely, for the door has a rather complicated lock, and is far from being an easy thing to manipulate."

"You know the terms of his will, then?" the Coroner inquired.

"Oh, yes," Everett said. "At present his niece, Miss Remsen, is his principal heir. There are many bequests to friends and to servants, but the bulk of the estate goes to Miss Remsen. Mr. Tracy knew that his marriage would invalidate this will, which was why he had not changed it. He said that after his wedding with Mrs. Dallas, he would revise the will to suite his changed estate."

"Then, under his existing will, Mrs. Dallas has no legacy?"

"Not unless Mr. Tracy made a change without telling me. He may have done that, but I think it very unlikely."

"You know of no one then, who had sufficient enmity toward Mr. Tracy to desire his death?"

"Absolutely no one. So far as I am aware, he hadn't an acquaintance in the world who was anything but friendly toward him."

Everett was dismissed and Billy Dean was called in.

He was a pleasant-faced chap of twenty-three or thereabouts. His work was far from being as important as Everett's. In fact he was really a high-class stenographer and office boy.

He was good looking with big brown eyes and a curly mop of brown hair. He too, scoffed at the idea of a secret passage in the house.

"Pleasure Dome has all the modern improvements," he said,

"but nothing like that. If there was such a thing, I'd have been through it in no time. I can ferret out anything queer of that sort by instinct, and there's nothing doing. There's no way in and out of Mr. Tracy's suite but by that one hall door. I know that. And it has a special lock. He had that put on about six months ago."

"Why? Was he afraid of intruders?"

"Don't think so. But there had been some robberies down in the village and he said it was as well to be on the safe side."

"Then, Mr. Dean, in your opinion, how did the man who killed Mr. Tracy get out of his rooms?"

"That's where you get me. I'm positively kerflummixed. I can't see anybody twisting that peculiar key with a bit of wire. Though that's easier to swallow than to imagine any one jumping out of the window."

"Why? The windows are not so very high."

"No. But the lake there is mighty deep and dangerous."

"Why specially dangerous?"

"Because there are swirling undercurrents, you see, it's almost like a caldron. That Sunless Sea, as Mr. Tracy named it, is in a cove and the winds make the water eddy about, and—well, I'm a pretty fair diver, but I wouldn't dive out of a second story window into that cove!"

"Then, we have to look for either a clever mechanician or an expert diver," said Keeley Moore. "How about the chauffeur?"

"He's an expert mechanician all right, but he wouldn't harm a hair of Mr. Tracy's head. He loved him, as, indeed, we all did. Nobody could help loving that man. He was always genial, courteous and kindly to everybody."

"And his niece, Miss Remsen?" asked the Coroner. "She, too, is gentle and lovely?"

Young Dean blushed fiery red.

"Yes, she is," was all he said, but no clairvoyance was needed to read his thoughts of her.

"Is she here?" asked Moore, knowing we had seen her arrive.

"Yes," Billy Dean said. "We telephoned her so soon as we knew what had happened, and she came right over."

"You may go now," said the Coroner, "and please send Miss Remsen in here."

CHAPTER V

THE LADY OF THE LAKE

"And so," I thought to myself, "I shall see again the Lady of the Lake."

As Alma Remsen entered the room, I realized the aptness of Kee's term, high-handed. Without any effect of strong-mindedness, the girl showed in face and demeanour a certain self-reliance, an air of determination, that made even a casual observer feel sure she could hold her own against all comers.

Yet she was a gentle sort. Slender, of medium height, with appealing brown eyes, she nodded a sort of greeting that included us all, and addressed herself to the coroner.

"You sent for me, Doctor Hart?" she said, in a low, musical voice.

"Yes, Miss Remsen. Will you answer a few direct questions?"

"Certainly. To the best of my ability."

"First of all, then, when did you last see your uncle alive?"

"I was over here day before yesterday, Tuesday, that would be. I have not been here since, until this morning."

My heart almost stopped beating. I had seen her come in her canoe—but stay, that was at one-thirty or thereabouts. Perhaps she salved her conscience for the lie by telling herself that was this morning.

"You mean, when you came over here perhaps half an hour ago?"

"Yes." Alma looked at him in some surprise. "What else could I mean?"

A finished actress, surely. I was amazed at her coolness and her pretty air of inquiry.

"Who summoned you?"

"Mrs. Fenn. She had been asked to do so by Mr. Ames."

"What was her message?"

"That Uncle Sampson had died of apoplexy and I'd better come right over."

"So you came?"

"Yes, as soon as I could get here."

"Have you seen—er—Mr. Tracy?"

"No; Mr. Ames advised against it."

"Well, Miss Remsen, I think we want no information from you, except a formal statement of your relationship to the dead man and your standing with him."

"Standing?"

"Yes. Were you good friends?"

"The best. I loved Uncle Sampson and he loved me, I know. I am his only living relative, except some distant cousins. I am the daughter of his sister, of whom he was very fond."

The girl was a bit of an enigma. She seemed straightforward and sincere, yet I was somehow conscious of a reservation in her talk, a glibness of speech that carried the idea of a prearranged story.

Why I should mistrust her I couldn't say, at first. Then I remembered that I had seen her canoeing over to Pleasure Dome in the night, and now she was saying she had not done so.

"Are you his heiress?" The question came sharply.

"So far as I know," she replied with perfect equanimity. "My uncle has told me that his will leaves the bulk of his estate to me, but he also told me that when he married Mrs. Dallas, he would revise that will, and make different arrangements."

"Did you resent this?"

"Not at all. I knew my uncle would leave me a proper portion of his wealth, and that as long as he lived he would take care of his sister's child."

"You are an only child of your parents?"

"I had a twin sister. She died fourteen years ago."

"And she is buried on this estate?"

"Her grave is in a small cemetery which also contains the graves of my parents and five or six other relatives of my uncle's family."

"How did it come about that the cemetery is on the grounds of the estate? It is, I believe, a New England custom."

"It was my mother's wish. She was devoted to the little girl who died and wanted to have the grave where she could visit it often. My uncle humoured her and also had the remains of my father sent here to be buried beside the child. Then, when my mother died, about a year ago, naturally she was buried there, too."

"I see. What did your sister die of?"

"Scarlet fever. There was an epidemic of it. We both had it, but I pulled through, though it left me with a slight deafness in one ear."

"Then, after your mother's death, you went to live by yourself on the island. Why did you do this?"

"Because my uncle was to marry Mrs. Dallas."

"And you don't like Mrs. Dallas?"

"I don't dislike her at all, but I am not of an easy-going disposition. I felt sure there would be clashes, and I told uncle I'd rather live by myself. He understood and agreed. So after some looking about, we decided on the island of Whistling Reeds as the most attractive site for a home."

"And he built a house for you there?"

"Oh, no, the house was already there. He bought the whole island, house and all."

"You like it as a home?"

"I love it. I am happier there than I could be anywhere else."

"Are you not lonely?"

"No more than I would be anywhere. I have capable and devoted servants, and I have tennis courts and an archery field and I have many boats and can get any place I wish to go in them. No, I am not so lonely as I sometimes was here in this great house. Of course, since my mother's death, I haven't gone much in society but I am thinking of going out more in the future."

Keeley Moore listened to the girl with the deepest interest. I wondered what he would say if he knew what I knew of her midnight canoe trip!

But I vowed to myself then and there that I should never tell of that. I knew I might be doing wrong, withholding such an important bit of information, but I was determined to keep my secret.

I tried to make myself think it was some other girl I had seen, but the alert figure before me and the white costume said plainly that I was making no mistake in recognizing the girl of the canoe.

From beneath her little white felt hat strayed a few golden curls, and I well remembered the bare head that had looked silvery in the moonlight.

I said to myself, by way of placating my conscience, that when the time came I would tell Kee about it, but I certainly did not propose to give the Coroner a chance to suspect this lovely girl of crime.

Apparently, the Coroner had no slightest suspicion of Alma, but you can't tell. He may have been drawing her out in order to prove her complete innocence or he may have felt that she had motive and must be closely questioned.

"Were you at home last evening?" Hart said, in a casual tone.

"Yes, I was."

"You didn't go out all the evening or night?"

"No. I didn't leave the island."

"Whew!" I exclaimed to myself, "it's lucky she doesn't know that I know!"

I gazed at her in admiration. I didn't, I couldn't think that she had killed her uncle, but knowing, as I did, that she had visited

Pleasure Dome, I could only think that she had come on some secret errand.

"Maybe," I puzzled over it, "she came to see her uncle on some private business, and saw the murderer at his work. Maybe she knew the criminal, and is shielding him."

For I had already made up my mind that some one in the house had killed Sampson Tracy. I didn't believe in any burglar or intruder. I thought a member of the family or household had done the deed, and, presumably, for the sake of inheritance. I had heard there were large bequests to the servants in Tracy's will, and there were several men to suspect.

I longed for a talk alone with Kee, but I saw this could not occur very soon.

"How did you occupy your evening?" pursued Hart, and I listened eagerly for the answer.

"I had an interesting book I was reading and after dinner I sat in my living room with the book until I finished the story. Then I played on the piano a little, as I often do in the evening, and about half-past ten I went to bed."

All of this was stated in a calm, even voice, and with the most clear and unflinching gaze of the brown eyes.

I realized then what beautiful eyes they were. Deep brown, with long, curling black lashes, and an expression of wistful appeal that would go straight to any man's heart.

Once for all, I was committed to the cause of Alma Remsen, and never, to Kee Moore or to anybody else, would I divulge any word that might make trouble for her.

I wasn't exactly in love with the girl then, or if I was I didn't know it. But I felt like a guardian toward her, and surely my first duty was to guard the secret of her canoe trip that night.

"You come over here often?" Moore asked, in his pleasant way, and she replied without hesitation.

"Oh, yes, I come over in my canoe or my motor boat nearly every day. Uncle gives me vegetables and fruit from the garden, and flowers, too."

"You say you haven't seen your uncle since his death," Kee went on. "Have you been told of the peculiar details of his deathbed?"

"Yes," Alma said, her brown eyes clouding with perplexity. "But I can't understand the meaning of such conditions. Who do you suppose would do such absurd things?"

"Doctor Rogers thinks it was the work of some small girl——"

"Ridiculous!" cried Alma. "Does he think a small girl killed my uncle?"

"No, apparently the deed was done by a strong man. But he

thinks the flowers and those things were put where they were found by some mischievous child. Do you know of any ten- or twelve-year-old girl near by?"

"No, I don't," and she looked about wonderingly. "Of course, there are lots of them in the village, but I know of none among the servants' families or in the neighbourhood at all. I don't agree with Doctor Rogers. It's too fantastic to think of a child coming along here at that time of night and getting into the house——Oh, the very idea is ridiculous."

"I agree to that," said Hart. "But how can we explain the feather duster and the food and all that?"

"I don't know, I'm sure," Alma declared, "but any man who was diabolically minded enough to drive a nail into the head of a sleeping victim would have a distorted brain, and might have done all those queer things. But cannot you detectives and policemen find out the truth?"

Her tone was appealing, she seemed to be asking their help, and I marvelled afresh at her poise and calm.

"You and Mrs. Dallas are friendly?" Coroner Hart broke out, abruptly.

"Oh, yes. We are not intimates, she is older than I am. But we have never had anything but the pleasantest of interviews."

"You are friendly with Mr. Ames?"

"In a general way, yes. He too, is so much older than I am that I have never given him a thought save as a friend of my uncle's. I don't know Mr. Ames very well, but I've certainly no unfriendly feelings toward him."

I wondered at myself. Why did I so admire this girl, so respect her, and yet have an undercurrent of fear for her? She was utterly frank, perfectly straightforward, to all appearances, yet—probably influenced by what I knew—I couldn't believe in her.

She was so self-possessed, so unafraid in her attitude and expression of face, that I had no real reason to doubt her good faith.

But I did, and I determined to watch Alma Remsen carefully and to the exclusion of everybody else connected with the mystery.

Moreover, I determined to keep my knowledge to myself. I wasn't sure whether I should tell Moore eventually or not, but at any rate, I wasn't ready to tell him yet.

After a few questions, which seemed to me of no real importance, Alma was excused and Mrs. Dallas was summoned.

What a different type of woman!

She was, as I learned later, about thirty, but her hair had turned prematurely gray, almost white. She wore it short, a soft, curly bob, that framed her young-looking face with a sort of halo.

Her eyes were gray, too, with dark lashes, and her complexion was perfect. That lovely creamy flesh, with a soft sheen on it that needed, I felt sure, no aid of cosmetics.

Her mouth was a Cupid's bow, and her smile was that of a siren.

I gazed at her, because I couldn't tear my eyes away.

True, I had seen her the night before at the Moores' dinner party, but she hadn't looked like this then. At the dinner she had seemed out of sorts, and unsmiling.

Now, she was animated and fascinating.

A strange idea came to me. Suppose she had killed Sampson Tracy, wouldn't she adopt this attitude of charm to wheedle the Coroner?

Then I laughed at my own foolishness. Why, of all people, would Katherine Dallas kill the man she was about to marry? The wealthy, powerful magnate, who was ready to dower her with everything heart could wish and put her at the head of his great establishment. Of course not. She had no motive, nor had she opportunity. Even if she possessed a latchkey, which might well be, she couldn't come to the house in the dead of night, and get away again, without being seen by somebody.

Although, I was forced to admit, whoever killed the man had gone to his room in the dead of night, and had got away again, unseen, so far as we could learn. How had he got away? Well, that question was as yet unanswered.

Even now, I realized, Coroner Hart was asking Mrs. Dallas her opinion on this very matter.

"I can't imagine," she said, and I was angry with myself to realize that her voice had in it no ring of a false note, no hint of insincerity.

"It is too impossible," she went on, her lovely face alight with interest, "whoever killed Mr. Tracy had to get out of that room and leave the door locked behind him, but how could he do it?"

"Dived out of the window," suggested Keeley, to hear what she would say.

"Then he was a master diver," she told him. "Deep Lake, or as they call it here, the Sunless Sea, is not only very deep, but it is full of hidden rocks and there are strong eddies and currents,—oh, it is a dangerous hole!"

"There's the alternative of a secret passage," Moore went on. "Did you ever hear of one?"

"No, and I doubt there being such. I mean, the house, though of complicated structure, is modern and I'm quite sure it hasn't any concealed or subterranean passages. If it had, I think Mr. Tracy would have spoken of them to me."

"Why do you feel so sure of that?"

"Only because he told me everything. I mean he was confidential by nature and I've never known him to have a secret from me."

"Why didn't Mr. Tracy attend the dinner last night at which you were a guest?"

She coloured a little, but answered frankly: "We had had a little tiff, and he was, while not really angry at me, just enough annoyed to stay home from the party. I think he regretted having declined the invitation, but then it was too late to change his mind."

"What was your disagreement about?"

"Must I tell that?"

"I think you'd better, Mrs. Dallas."

"I greatly prefer not to."

"Still I must request it."

"Well, then, he had said he wanted to tell me something about his niece, Miss Remsen."

"Something unpleasant?"

"I feared so. I didn't know. But he said it was a thing I ought to know about if I was coming into the family."

"He gave you no hint as to the purport of his disclosures?"

"He wanted to, but I wouldn't listen. I told him I didn't want to hear it, at any rate, not then."

"Why did you take that attitude in the matter?"

"I'll try to explain. I have known Mr. Tracy about a year. I've been engaged to him about three months. Now, he had never mentioned this thing before. So I had a feeling that he had spoken impulsively, and perhaps on thinking it over would change his mind about telling me."

"And you had no curiosity about it?"

"Oh, no, not beyond a natural wonder as to what it could be. But I am very fond of Alma Remsen, and I was positive it couldn't be anything really serious. Perhaps an early love affair or escapade that would be better left buried in oblivion."

"So you had words over it all."

"Yes, I was so insistent that he should not tell me, and he so equally insistent that I should hear it, that we had a real quarrel."

"How did it wind up?"

"By his leaving my house—he was calling on me—in a rage. I admit it was a foolish thing to quarrel about, but I was determined to have my way in the matter, and I did."

"When was this affair?"

43

"It was Monday night."

"And to-day is Thursday. You didn't see him again?"

"No. He sulked Tuesday and Wednesday. I called him on the telephone yesterday and asked him if he was going to the Moores' dinner party, and he said 'No,' very shortly and hung up the receiver."

"He was really angry, then?"

"Yes, but I fancy more with himself than with me. Mr. Ames told me that Mr. Tracy was sorry about it all, and that he kept my scarf near him all the time. I know Mr. Tracy's ways, and when he keeps any of my belongings near him, he isn't really angry at me."

"You are speaking of the crimson scarf that was found on Mr. Tracy's bed?"

"Yes, that one." And then, the calm of Katherine Dallas broke down and she burst into a piteous flood of tears.

I was not surprised. I had noticed her clenching fingers and her tapping foot, and I knew she was striving to keep a grip on her feelings.

It was Inspector Farrell who opened the door for her, and as she stumbled through, we saw Alma Remsen awaiting her, and knew she would be duly cared for.

Farrell returned into the room and closed the door, and went slowly back to his seat.

"What about it?" he said, including both Hart and Keeley Moore in his glance of inquiry.

"Whoever killed that man, it was not Mrs. Dallas," Kee declared. "I don't suppose anybody thought she did, but there's no slightest reason to suspect her."

"What about the girl?" asked Farrell, with brooding eyes.

"Drive a nail in her uncle's head!" Moore exclaimed. "I can't see her doing that! Can you, Norris?"

"No," I said, and it was God's truth. That lovely girl connected with a brutal, inhuman deed,—no, nobody could believe that!

"Well, then, where are we at?" Farrell asked.

"At Harper Ames," said the coroner, and we realized that he was sticking to his first impressions.

"All right," Farrell sighed. "Get him in here next, then."

But just then, Sally Bray came to the door. Farrell let her in and asked the result of her investigation of Mr. Tracy's belongings.

"There's nothing missing as Griscom and I can see," she reported, "except two things—I mean, three."

"What are they?" and Farrell placed a chair for her and spoke in a kindly tone.

"One is the Tottum Pole."

44

"The what?"

"She doubtless means the Totem Pole," said Moore, quietly. "Is that it, Sally?"

"Yes, sir, that's what I said, the Tottum Pole. It was one of Mr. Tracy's favourite toys. It was Indian, Griscom says, and it always stood on his bedside table. He thought it was a—a charm, like."

"A Luck you mean, I dare say." Keeley had taken the inquiry into his own hands for the moment.

"Yes, sir, it was his Luck, that's what Griscom said."

"How large was it?"

"About so big." Sally measured a foot or more with her hands. "Oh, it was fierce! Yet beautiful, too."

"Bright colours, and a face at the top——"

"Yes, sir. But a norful face, all eyes——"

"I know. You understand, Mr. Farrell, don't you? She means a miniature Totem Pole. They have them in the better class of shops round here that carry Indian trinkets. The little Totem Poles are interesting, and are called lucky. I have two or three at home. But mine are smaller, only six or eight inches. And so this Totem Pole is missing. What else, Sally?"

"Two of Mr. Tracy's best weskits, sir! His striped dark blue morey, and his pearl-coloured figgered satin."

"He wore fancy waistcoats, then?"

"Oh, yes, sir, he was a great hand for weskits of beautiful stuff. Never gay or gaudy, but soft, lovely colours and the expensivest materials."

"And two of them are gone. Are you sure?"

"Yes, sir. Griscom missed 'em. He says they ain't gone to the cleaner's or anything like that, for they're both nearly new. And he says he knows they were in their right place yesterday morning, sir."

"Well," Hart said, "we can't complain of any lack of curious complications. This seems to prove a man did the deed. A woman surely would not take fancy waistcoats!"

"And why should a man take them, either?" Moore asked, but none of us could answer.

CHAPTER VI

THE WATCH IN THE WATER PITCHER

"Well, Sally, is that all?"

"No, sir, not quite. Griscom found one more queer thing. He found Mr. Tracy's watch in the water pitcher."

"In the water pitcher!" Farrell exclaimed. "Was there water in the pitcher?"

"Oh, yes, sir, it was nearly full. And down at the bottom of it was the watch."

"How extraordinary. Is the watch going?"

"I don't know, sir. Griscom took it out of the pitcher, but I don't know what he did with it."

"Well, we'll see about it. If you've no more astonishing bits of information, you can run along, Sally."

The girl left the room, and we looked at one another, half smiling, half appalled.

"It's all so tawdry," Keeley Moore said, with an impatient shrug of his shoulders.

"Just what meaning do you attach to the word 'tawdry'?" asked Hart. "I can't seem to make it apply at all."

"Oh, I only mean these foolish clues that some practical joker has arranged are tawdry of intent. I may be obliged to change my mind, but just at present, I can't think that the person who killed Sampson Tracy is the person who stuck the feather duster behind his head and dropped his watch in the water pitcher. By the way, why did he have a water pitcher, with an elaborate bathroom at hand?"

"Call Griscom, let's find out a little more about it."

So the butler came at a summons, and explained that the water pitcher was a pitcher of drinking water that was placed on a table for him every night.

"Mr. Tracy didn't approve of thermos bottles," Griscom informed us. "He said they never seemed clean things to him. So he had a pitcher."

"When you found the watch, was it running?"

"No, sir, it was not."

"At what time had it stopped?"

Inspector Farrell awaited the answer with an air of one expecting a piece of important information. But he was disappointed.

46

"I didn't exactly notice, sir, but it isn't the watch Mr. Tracy was carrying. That is still under his pillow. This watch I found in the pitcher is an old one, and it was lying on his dressing table last night."

"Why was it there?"

"Mr. Tracy had it out, looking at it a day or two ago. He thought he would send it to a jeweller and have it put in order. The mainspring is broken, you see. But he didn't decide, and the watch lay there, in a little tray, with some other odds and ends of jewellery."

"Then, somebody took that watch and deliberately dropped it into the water pitcher?"

"That must be the truth, sir."

"Mr. Tracy never showed the slightest disposition toward any mental affection, did he?"

"Oh, no, indeed, sir. Nothing of that sort."

"Who do you think killed Mr. Tracy, Griscom?"

Farrell shot this question so suddenly that I was not surprised to see the butler turn pale and grasp at the chair in front of him to steady himself.

"I—I don't know, sir."

"Of course you don't know. I'm asking you what you think."

"Well, what can I think, but Mr. Ames."

"Mr. Ames! Why would he do such a thing?"

"Well, sir, it had to be somebody with motive. Mr. Ames had that, and likewise opportunity."

"You've been reading detective stories. You're very glib with your 'motive and opportunity'! How could Mr. Ames get in?"

"He carries a latchkey, sir."

"I don't mean into the house, I mean in the room, Mr. Tracy's room."

"Well, the door wasn't always locked at night. About half the time it was left unlocked."

"Then, how could he get out after the deed and leave the door locked on the inside?"

"That's more than I can tell you. I thought that's what you detectives were going to explain. But kill my master somebody did, and get out of the room, he did, too. So there must be an explanation somewhere."

"A secret passage, I suppose."

"No, sir. I'm ready to swear there's no secret passage in this house."

"You may not know of it."

"Well, sir, how could there be? That wing of Mr. Tracy's is

foursquare. It has no L's or bays. You can measure it up and you'll find there's no bit of space unaccounted for. The rooms open into one another, and there's just the wall between, no room for a concealed staircase."

"How are you so sure? You been examining around?"

"Just that, sir, meaning no harm. But I somehow feel I've got to find out the truth of this whole thing, and so I've got to look into the conditions."

Keeley Moore gave Griscom a stare of decided interest. It was evident he thought the man knew rather more than he had credited him with.

Farrell and Hart were not so well pleased, apparently. They frowned a little, and the Inspector advised the butler not to exceed his orders or overstep his privileges.

And then it was lunch time, and Keeley, remembering his wife's hint of blackberry shortcake, decided we must go home at once.

"I want to think matters over a bit," he said to the police officers. "If you want me here, I will come when summoned, but otherwise I'll stay at home this afternoon. When will you have the inquest, Doctor Hart?"

"To-morrow," said the Coroner. "Though it will probably have to be adjourned. I confess I'm in a quandary. I scarcely know which way to look. You know I am relying on your help, Mr. Moore."

"I'll help all I can," Kee said, gravely. "But I think you've got a hard nut to crack."

"You mean the locked room——"

"No, I don't mean the locked room. That will explain itself, once you get the criminal."

"Then you mean all these bizarre clues we have to deal with."

"No, I don't mean those, either. The finding of the criminal will wipe those out at once. It's the hunt that is hard. The quarry is elusive and hard to track. Find the motive first; that's always a sound plan."

And with that Moore and I went off, leaving behind us a greatly perplexed pair of sleuths of the law.

A car belonging to the house conveyed us home, and by good luck we were not late for luncheon.

The shortcake materialized and proved worthy of all praise, and Kee refused to talk about the tragedy at all until the meal was over and we gathered in the lounge afterward.

Lora and Maud had heard only scraps of information from neighbours and tradesmen, but they had not been inquisitive, preferring to wait until we returned to tell them all about it.

And so the four of us sat down for a real confab.

48

I listened while Keeley told his wife all the information he had so far accumulated, and I couldn't help admiring the straightforward, clean-cut story he told. He might have been a skilled reporter, giving the known facts to the public.

Of course my conscience pricked me because I was holding back the very important bit of evidence that I seemed the only one to know. Apparently no one but myself had seen Alma Remsen go in her canoe to Pleasure Dome the night before at about half past one o'clock.

I might be accessory after the fact. I might be aiding and abetting a criminal, but, shameless that I was, I didn't care, and had no intention of telling my secret.

My justification, adequate in my own mind, was that I didn't for a minute believe Alma Remsen had killed her uncle. It was too incredible, too impossible. Go to his house, she did. Stay there about an hour, she did. But kill him, no! Perhaps she saw the deed committed, perhaps she arrived later, and saw the dead victim, perhaps—a very doubtful perhaps—she arranged the bizarre decorations, but strike the deadly blow—never!

So, I felt I had a right to keep still about the matter, for why drag the girl into detestable prominence, and have her wrongly suspected of crime, when all I had to do was to keep silence?

Lora listened quietly, with sundry intelligent nods of her head, and Maud Merrill was no less interested. I had great respect for the intelligence of both these women, and listened eagerly for their comments.

"Too many suspects," said Lora, as Kee finished his recital.

"Yes," agreed Maud, "there's positively nobody in the house outside suspicion."

"Then we must eliminate," said Kee.

"We can't exactly eliminate," Lora told him, "but we can guess who had the strongest motive."

"Guess!"

"That's all we can do. I can't see that there are any clues that mean anything. All those flowers and things were already in the room. As clues, they all go for nothing. The murderer was not necessarily a man of fantastic tastes or a child of playful tendencies, he only cut up those tricks so we would think he was."

"That's right," Kee said. "It wasn't even specially clever. He just picked up anything he saw about and laid it on the bed to fog things up. So what about motive? I can't imagine any one wanting to kill Tracy for anything except a sordid reason. Money, I am sure, is the only motive."

"Love?" I said. "Was no one else enamoured of the beautiful Mrs. Dallas, and wanted Tracy out of the way?"

"Of course, Charlie Everett adored her," Lora said, "but he wouldn't commit murder to get her. And if he did, he wouldn't choose such a horrible, brutal method. He'd shoot his victim, not assassinate him with a hammer and nail!"

"I think that, too," Kee declared. "To my mind, that nail business indicates a low type of personality. A servant seems the most likely. Griscom, for choice."

Now I knew Keeley Moore well enough to know that if he suggested Griscom, Griscom was not the man he suspected. He had a way of drawing out other people, by hints and allusions, in hope of getting a side light on his own suspect.

"If the motive was to achieve at once the legacy from the Tracy estate, then every inmate of that house is suspect. Farrell told me that Mr. Tracy's will left a substantial bequest to each of the servants, to the secretary and to Mr. Ames," I told my audience.

"All right," exclaimed Moore, "let's begin at the top. What have we got against Harper Ames?"

"His immediate need for money, his hateful, belligerent disposition, his love for Mrs. Dallas and his unhampered opportunity," I declared, promptly.

"I thought he was a woman hater," cried Maud Merrill. "Why do you say he was in love with her?"

"I may not be a detective," I said, "but I am not entirely a nincompoop. When I saw those two people here last evening, I realized that whatever he calls himself, he's no woman hater where Mrs. Dallas is concerned. He adores her; in the language of the poet, he worships the ground she walks on."

"Norris is right about that," Keeley conceded. "I've seen it for some time. And when these avowed woman haters fall for a siren, they fall hard. Yes, Ames is head over ears in love with the lady, and for that very reason, he's out of the running. A man isn't going to commit murder to win a lady's hand. It's too dangerous a proceeding. If Ames were not in love with her, I might suspect him."

"But, hold on, Kee. There might be circumstances," I said, "in which Ames lost his head, or his temper, or both, and let fly at Tracy in an ungovernable fit of rage——"

"That murder wasn't done in an ungovernable fit of rage, it was a premeditated affair. Whoever did it, came prepared with that nail and a hammer——"

"Why a hammer?" I demanded. "The nail could have been driven in with any heavy object."

"Such as what?"

50

I ruminated over the appointments of the room as I remember them, and said, a little lamely, "Well, one could take off his shoe to drive the nail."

"Yes, one could," Kee assented, "but it doesn't sound likely——"

"The whole affair doesn't sound likely," I countered, "and anyway, it doesn't matter. Somebody did drive that nail, and what it was driven with is unimportant. As far as I can learn, they've found nothing conclusive in the way of fingerprints. I'm not keen on those things myself, but in New York they would have been fingerprinting the whole crowd of us."

"Of course, there are no available fingerprints on the nail," Kee said, "and that's the only thing that matters. I don't give a fig for all the feather dusters, flowers, oranges and such things."

"Not even the watch in the water pitcher?" I asked.

"Well, yes, I do consider the watch in the water pitcher. In fact, I think that's the key note of the whole performance."

"You've got to tell us why," I told him. "You can't say that and leave it unexplained."

"Indeed I can. A real detective never explains his cryptic utterances."

"You're not a real detective," I declared, solemnly.

"Why not?" and he glowered at me.

"Because you look like a detective. You're tall, and dark and hawk-eyed or hawk-nosed, or hawk-somethinged. Now, a real detective must always look utterly unlike the detective of fiction, and you're the very image of Sherlock Holmes."

"And I glory in it. But if you flatter yourself you're my Watson, you must cultivate the ornament of a meek and quiet spirit."

"I thought we were eliminating," put in Maud. "Who have we eliminated so far?"

"Your English is deplorable," Kee told her, "but I can deduce your meaning. Well, how about eliminating Ames?"

"No," I cried, "he's the one not to eliminate. There are too many counts against him. I say, let's begin at the other end of the line. The lesser servants."

"Cut out Sally Bray, then," Moore advised. "That girl never had the nerve to go a-murdering all by herself."

"Of course not," I agreed. "Though she may have gone with some companion."

"No, it isn't plausible. As to the servants, all we can say is that they could have had opportunity. The house servants, at any rate, could have had a duplicate key made to the Tracy suite——"

"But that wasn't needed. So far as we know the door wasn't

locked when the murderer went in. But he left it locked when he came out."

"That's the point of the whole thing," Lora said, confidently. "You can't do this elimination you talk about, for every servant had a motive, if you count greed a motive, and 'every servant had a chance to get into the room unnoticed. Now it all comes back to the explanation of the intruder leaving the door locked behind him. Give me a possible explanation, Kee."

"There are but two," he said, thoughtfully. "I am sure there's no secret passage, for I measured and sounded the walls thoroughly. So it's either that the criminal had some clever mechanical contrivance with which he turned that key in the door behind him, or he jumped out of the window."

"Into the lake!" cried Lora.

"Yes, into the lake. It implies an expert diver, and it is a most dangerous proceeding, even then. But you asked for the possibilities."

"Is Everett or Dean an expert diver?" I asked.

"Everett is. Dean not."

"And Everett is in love with the Dallas, too. Well, we can hardly eliminate him, then."

"But I refuse to suspect a lover of murder," Kee insisted. "He must realize he will be suspected, if not convicted, and where would he stand with the fair one then?"

"Murderers don't always think ahead," I said, sagely.

"This one did. He thought far enough ahead to bring that horrible nail. We've no reason to think there was a nail lying about among the flowers and crackers."

"Isn't there a story about somebody being killed with a nail?" I asked.

"There is," Kee replied, "it's in Holy Writ. Jael killed Sisera, or Sisera killed Jael, I forget which, but the weapon was a nail driven in the victim's head."

"Yes," I returned, "I know, but I don't mean that story. There's another—by a Frenchman——"

"No," said Maud, in her quiet, confident way, "it's a Spanish story, by Pedro de Alarcón. The name of it is The Nail. It's a horrible tale, but the theme is a murder by a nail driven in a man's head."

"Then," and Kee shook himself, as if roused to action, "then we must look for a man who has read that story. Nobody would think of a nail, unless something had suggested it to him. I say that eliminates all the servants, unless, maybe, that chauffeur chap, Louis. I can't see any of the others reading Spanish stories, even in

52

translation. Item one. Search the Tracy library for a copy of that story. Is it a whole book, Maud?"

"No. A short story. I read it in a collection of Spanish and Italian mystery tales. I have it at home, but there's no point to it in connection with this matter, except the nail."

"That association means something," Kee persisted. "When we do find the murderer, we'll find he got his notion from that story."

"Or from the Bible," I said.

"Maybe. But I think more likely Maud's story. As I remember it, the Scripture narrative is not very dramatic, and so, less likely to imbue our murderer's mind with the plan than the Spanish yarn is."

"Granting the Spanish story, then," I said, "can't we eliminate the servants? They'd surely not read such literature."

"All right, eliminate them for the moment," Kee agreed. "We can always go back to them if need be. That leaves us, in the house, Everett, Billy Dean and Ames. Help yourself."

"Ames," I said decidedly. "He's the very one to read morbid, sensational literature."

"But everybody reads detective stories nowadays," Lora said. "Especially the grave and reverend seigneurs who wouldn't be suspected of such tastes."

"This wasn't a detective story," Maud informed us. "It was a thriller, a scare story."

"All the same," I said, "and more in line with Ames's effects than straight detective yarns. I'm all for Ames. He wanted money, a lot of money, and Tracy wouldn't let him have it, so, as he would not only get a large bequest at Tracy's death, but, for all we know, could bury in oblivion his indebtedness to Tracy, of course he wanted Tracy out of the way. Moreover, if by the same token he could get the beautiful lady, that was an added inducement."

"I'm ready to admit all that," Kee was very thoughtful now; "and I can conceive of Ames in a murderer's rôle. But I happen to know he is no diver. He can swim a little, but not expertly, and he can scarcely dive at all."

"Perhaps," I offered, "he is a master-diver, and had kept it secret for this very reason. What do you know of his past?"

"Nothing at all. And Norris, that was clever of you. If Harper Ames came here to commit that murder and escape by the window, it would be in keeping with his diabolical astuteness to pretend to be inexpert at swimming."

"We're building up a case instead of eliminating," I said, secretly elated at Moore's word of praise. "But before we go on, what about the two secretaries? I mean, are they omnivorous readers?"

"Mr. Everett is," Maud volunteered. "He was here one night and

53

we talked about books. We didn't talk very seriously, but I gathered he was widely read, and had really good taste in literature."

"And Everett is undoubtedly in love with Mrs. Dallas," Kee went on, "and of course, he will have a bequest, and of course, he could get out of the room as well as anybody else, and we know somebody did, so all things being equal, why not suspect Everett instead of Ames?"

"Because of the difference in the characters of the two men," Lora said, with emphasis. "I'm ready to grant a murderer may masquerade as an angel of light, but all the same, we have to judge our fellow men more or less by appearances, and I'll pick Ames for a criminal long before I'll choose Charlie Everett."

"And we're leaving out Billy Dean entirely?"

"I am," I said. "He's a nice, decent chap, and he's too young for a murderer, at least, with no motive other than a bit of money. He isn't in love with Mrs. Dallas, is he?"

"Lord, no. He's in love with the Remsen girl."

"Well, then," I said, "if that nice boy is in love with that nice girl, he's not going to commit a crime. I say, let's eliminate him."

"Then," Kee summed up, "we've eliminated everybody but Ames and Everett. Griscom is the only servant we could possibly suspect, and he is said to be devoted to his master, and too, I'm told he has a tidy sum laid by, so I don't see him driving nails into people."

"We can't get away from the nail and the sort of character it connotes," I said. "I stand by Ames until he's definitely eliminated."

"Well, I guess we're all agreed, then," and Keeley rose and stretched his long arms. "Now, I'm for a swim. Who'll go?"

We all went, and I found that the water of a sunny cove of Deep Lake was an ideal bathtub, and I forgot for the time being the sinister depths of the Sunless Sea.

CHAPTER VII

THE INQUEST

The inquest was an interesting affair.

I gathered from Coroner Hart's manner that he had picked up some information or some bits of evidence that meant a lot to him, and he seemed impatient to begin his questioning.

The setting of the scene was far too beautiful to be wasted on a crime session and I looked about at the curious crowd of neighbours and villagers with distaste.

We were in the great ballroom, which occupies the lower floor of the wing containing Sampson Tracy's rooms. On three sides, the Sunless Sea lapped its dark waters against its rocky shores, and the merest glance into its black depths was enough to deter the stoutest heart from an unnecessary dive therein. But an escaping murderer, if brave enough to risk the danger, and skilled enough in diving and sufficiently familiar with the position of the principal rocks, might make the goal. It was a comfort to me to think that, since the authorities assumed that was the way the criminal got out, it rather freed Alma Remsen from suspicion.

For that delicate girl, even though a good diver, as I had heard, could never have committed that brutal murder, and then have dived into those perilous depths at desperate risk of her own life.

Seats had been reserved for our crowd, and as we took them I glanced at the coroner's jury. All well to do and fine looking men from the large estates that bordered the whole length of Deep Lake. Some were grave, some seemed unable to quell a naturally gay and jolly disposition, but all were alert and alive, and I felt that the case was in good hands.

I knew few of the audience. Mrs. Dallas was accompanied by several friends, and I also noted the young girl, Posy May, who had been at the Moores' dinner party.

Then I saw Alma Remsen. She sat near Posy and she was accompanied by a woman who impressed me strongly. Never have I seen a face of more determination and grim endurance than that of Mrs. Merivale, which I later learned was her name.

She was the nurse who had cared for Alma since she was born. She lived with the girl in her island home, and surely no one could ask for a more capable and efficient-looking guardian.

Not a fine lady, but beyond all doubt a fine woman, Mrs. Merivale was tall and gaunt of figure and possessed a large, bony face whose stern, set mouth was belied by a touch of humour quite evident in the shrewd gray eyes.

But what most impressed me was her expression of wisdom. Surely, this was a woman to whom all the experiences of life were as an open book. She had the look of a witch or sibyl, although her gray hair was decorously smooth beneath her small black hat.

She noted every new arrival, she swept the jury with her all-seeing glance and finally concentrated her attention on the coroner, until, with a quick nod of satisfaction, she ended that scrutiny.

Then she turned a little to contemplate the girl beside her.

Alma Remsen, to-day in a costume of soft beige-coloured silk weave, looked nervous and worried. Her golden hair, escaping at the sides from her close little hat, framed a face that was clearly worn and wan from a sleepless night. At least it seemed that way to me, and I longed to tell her her secret was safe with me. Never would I divulge to any one the fact that she visited Pleasure Dome on the night of the tragedy. So far, I hadn't heard a hint of such a thing, and I hoped there would be none.

Though we hadn't been formally introduced, and I had never had a word of conversation with her, I nodded a greeting and smiled.

She inclined her head in slight acknowledgment, and then, to my amazement, a look of fright crossed her face.

I tried to persuade myself that she had seen some one else or heard some word that alarmed her, but in my heart I felt sure that the shadow of fear was caused by the sight of me.

What could it mean? I saw her slip her hand into that of the nurse beside her, and I noted the reassuring pat the woman gave her.

It seemed to comfort the girl, and she gave a little smile at her companion.

Not wanting to embarrass her further I turned my glance toward Mrs. Dallas. She looked superb this morning. Garbed all in black, yet a black that hinted Paris in its every line and fold, her beautiful face and her great gray eyes showed a quiet sadness that spoke of a deeper grief than emotion could show.

Her lovely gray hair was tucked under a black hat, and her lips and cheeks, quite evidently the result of a well-equipped vanity box, were the only touch of colour about her.

She sat between Harper Ames and Charles Everett, the post of chief mourner seemingly accorded her as her right.

Yet though she was calm and composed, it seemed to me there was an undercurrent of anxiety, a hint of dread or apprehension.

Nor was this to be wondered at. The occasion was a tragic one, and as the person most deeply affected by the tragedy, it was only natural that Katherine Dallas should be nervous.

Hart first questioned the servants. Though new matter to the jury, we had heard their stories before, and no fresh fact or bit of evidence was forthcoming.

No articles had been missed from Sampson Tracy's rooms except two of his fancy waistcoats and the gayly painted Totem Pole.

Several of the servants testified as to Mr. Tracy's previous possession of these three articles and of their unaccountable absence at present.

None of them had heard any sounds during the night or could throw any light on the mystery of the criminal's entrance or exit, if, indeed, he was not an inmate of the house.

All testified to the kindness and generosity of the master, and though all inherited a sum of money by his will, there seemed no real reason to suspect that any one of them had hastened the demise.

As Doctor Rogers was absent, Hart himself was the only one to give the medical report, and he told the jury succinctly and clearly the details of the death and how both doctors had thought it apoplexy at first, as the symptoms were of such an attack.

"Without doubt, the autopsy would have disclosed the truth," Hart said, "but before that, Mr. Moore, the famous New York City detective, noticed there was a tiny metal disk visible through the hair of the dead man. Investigation proved this to be the head of a nail, about two inches long, that had been driven with great force into Mr. Tracy's skull, presumably while he was alive and asleep."

"Could a nail be so driven, through the bone?" asked a mild mannered juryman.

"Yes," the coroner told him. "It would require a heavy driving instrument, and a strong hand, as well as a callous brain, for a man to accomplish that fiendish deed."

The bizarre decorations on the bed were then told about, and reference made to the watch found in the water pitcher and the absence of the plate that had held the fruit and the crackers. But these things were merely touched on, for the jury had only to discover the cause of the death, and these details were of slight help.

Individual testimony was another matter, and I felt a deep interest as Harper Ames was called to the stand.

I could see Keeley Moore also eager to learn what the visitor of the house would have to say.

Ames was in grumpy mood, as usual. More, he seemed belligerent, and I wondered whether the Coroner would try to placate him or would ruffle him still more.

"Will you state, in your own words, Mr. Ames, the circumstances of your return to this house, after a dinner party on Wednesday night?"

The question sounded abrupt, and, perhaps for that reason, it seemed to rouse Ames's resentment.

"That's about all there is to tell," he declared, frowning. "I came home from a dinner party next door, about eleven o'clock. I chatted with Mr. Tracy for a while and then we both went upstairs to bed. That's all."

He glared about him, as if he were being imposed on to have to testify at all. I tried to analyze the man. He had been insistent that Keeley Moore should take the case. Was this a gigantic bluff? I mean, could it be that Ames was himself the murderer, and sought to escape suspicion by frankly asking the detective to solve the mystery? Did he think he had so covered his tracks that he was safe from even the astute cleverness of Keeley Moore?

If this were the case, he was greatly mistaken. I had no idea whether Ames was the murderer or not, but if so, then he stood no chance of escaping the detection of my friend.

But Hart was proceeding, in a suave, pleasant way, calculated to soothe Ames's antagonism.

"You were Mr. Tracy's best friend?" he asked.

"That's saying a great deal, but I was certainly one of them. We have known each other from boyhood, and though we bandied words now and then, we never had a real quarrel in our lives."

"You owed him money?"

Harper Ames's eyes flashed, and he seemed about to fly into a rage. Then, apparently thinking better of it, he calmed down and said, quietly, but sullenly still:

"Yes, though I don't know that it's your business. Tracy has let me owe him money for a long time, and as he had no objections to it, I can't see your right to inquire about it."

"Yes, I have a right," Hart said, "and I propose to use it. How much did you owe him?"

"Some thousands," and now Ames's frown became a real scowl.

"And his will gives you a bequest of many thousands. It is a fortunate occurrence for you."

I thought and still think that Harper Ames had a right to get angry at the Coroner. If Hart suspected his witness he should have said so, and not cast these innuendoes at him.

Yet Ames said nothing. He contented himself with such a venomous glance of hatred at the Coroner, that I shivered at the sight. Keeley Moore, too, looked amazed at the way things were going. Then we both realized that this was doubtless Hart's first murder case. Such things didn't often happen up here in the peaceful lake region, and the sudden responsibility and authority had rather gone to Hart's head and made him a little uncertain of procedure.

Next he flung out the query, "Are you a good diver?"

At this Ames gave a sardonic smile.

"No," he returned, "I am not. To begin with I didn't kill Sampson Tracy, I didn't jump out of the window of his locked room, and I didn't bedeck his bed with flowers and ornaments. If these are the things you want to know, I am telling you."

"Yes," and the Coroner's air was imperturbable, "but I have only your unsupported word for all that."

Harper Ames stared at him as if he would like to drive a nail into his half-witted head, and then, drawing himself up with a new dignity, he said:

"That is true, Mr. Coroner. But I can't bring forward any witnesses to prove my statements. That is why I have been trying to engage the services of the famous Mr. Moore to take on this case, and to discover the true murderer of Sampson Tracy, for only such a course will prove the innocence of other suspects."

This was fine talk, but to me it didn't ring true. If Ames had done the foul deed himself, he might have put forth this very line of argument. He might have demanded the services of a great detective, feeling sure nobody could detect his guilt.

Well, it wasn't up to me to decide these things.

A few more inquiries of small importance finished up Ames's testimony and then Mrs. Dallas was questioned.

She was dignified of appearance and calm of speech. She said she was the fiancée of Mr. Tracy and they had expected to be married in the fall. She said they occasionally had little differences, but always made them up and were really very fond of one another. Her statements were all rational and straightforward. She spoke as might a cultured and mature woman of her accepted suitor.

Asked as to the terms of Mr. Tracy's will, she replied that so far as she knew his fortune was left to his niece, Miss Remsen. But, she added, he had told her that after they were married, he would change his will and make suitable arrangements for his wife. She said she had given the matter no thought, knowing that Mr. Tracy would do what was right.

This seemed to remove from her any possible suspicion that might have formed in the minds of the jury. Surely, Mrs. Dallas had no reason to kill the man she loved and expected to marry.

No reference was made to the disagreement the engaged pair

had had, and which had resulted in Mr. Tracy's absence from the Moores' dinner party.

I rejoiced at this, for I dreaded to have Alma's name brought in at all. But as I thought it over, I became a little alarmed. Had Hart omitted the point in order to tax Alma herself with it later? To ask her what was the tale her uncle desired to tell Mrs. Dallas? To see if it could be some disgraceful story that might militate against the girl herself?

The two secretaries followed Mrs. Dallas.

Everett, quiet-mannered and polite, as always, answered questions readily enough, but offered no additional information.

He repeated his story of the evening, how he had been with Mr. Tracy until about ten o'clock, and then had gone to his room and to bed.

"You heard no unusual sounds during the night?"

"No," said Everett, but it seemed to me he had hesitated.

Hart must have noticed this, too, for he said, "Are you quite sure? No sounds inside the house or out?"

Apparently Charlie Everett was a truthful man. But it was equally evident he did not want to testify further.

"I must press you for an answer, Mr. Everett," the Coroner prodded him.

"Well, to be strictly accurate, I may say that I thought I heard the sound of a boat on the lake some time after midnight."

"What sort of boat?"

"I don't know. And it may not have been any. I was asleep, and I partially awaked and seemed to hear a slight sound as of paddles. But it may well be that I dreamed it, for I heard no further sounds."

"Do you know the time this happened?"

"No, except that I seemed to have been asleep some hours. I thought nothing of it, and directly went to sleep again."

"You didn't look out of the window?"

"No, I didn't rise from my bed."

I thanked my lucky stars that he hadn't! That he hadn't seen Alma Remsen, in her canoe, some time after midnight!

But if the Coroner thought much about this bit of evidence he gave no sign of doing so, and the rest of the inquiries he put to Everett were of a stereotyped sort and led nowhere.

Then came Billy Dean. That cheerful young man was chipper as always and told all he had to tell in a clear and concise way.

"Did you hear any sound in the night as of a passing boat?" Hart asked him.

"No," Dean declared, and his voice was steady and all would

have been well but that the silly chap turned brick red from the roots of his hair to the top of his collar.

"Then," said Hart, with a full intention of embarrassing him, "why are you blushing like a turkey cock?"

"I'm not!" Dean stormed at him, getting redder yet. "But you barge into me with sudden questions and it knocks me off my base."

Clever! His winning smile and his sudden carrying of the war into the enemy's quarters succeeded, as I was sure he had hoped, in diverting the jury's attention from his palpable mendacity.

"Then you heard no boat?" Hart went back to his subject.

"I heard a motor boat, but that was about twelve o'clock," Dean said, reminiscently. "I heard none later, for I went to sleep then."

He had himself perfectly in hand, now, and though I confidently believed he had seen Alma Remsen in her canoe, I knew, too, that wild horses couldn't drag the fact from him.

"And you heard no further noises?"

"Not till morning, when Everett rapped on my door, and told me to get up."

There seemed to be nothing more to get out of young Dean, and he was dismissed. He had made a good effect on the jury, I could see that. Since they didn't have my knowledge of the girl in the boat, they were not greatly interested in the vague sounds mentioned by Everett.

In fact, I could gather from the whole trend of the inquest that suspicion centred on the inmates of the house. There was little thought given to the outer world.

Then Alma Remsen was called.

Without asking permission, Mrs. Merivale rose and went with her charge to the witness chair. She took another chair beside Alma, and her big, hard face looked like a tower of strength, should such be needed.

"You were not at this house on Wednesday evening or night at any time?" the Coroner said. It was more a statement than a question, and it sounded to me as if Hart wanted to shut up this point once and for all.

"No, I was not," Alma replied, and I hoped nobody except me noticed the quivering of her eyelids.

That was the only way she showed any nervousness. Her hands lay quietly in her lap, her lips were not trembling, her eyes were clear and steady in their gaze, but the eyelids fluttered once, twice, as if she was holding herself together by sheer force of will.

"Where were you that evening?"

"At home, in my own house."

"All the evening?"

"Yes."

"Who is your companion?"

"Mrs. Merivale. My housekeeper and friend."

"Will she corroborate your presence in your home?"

Hart's voice was most courteous, but it also was decided.

"Surely," said Alma. "Will you question her?"

"Miss Remsen was at home all Wednesday evening?" he said.

"Yes, sir," the woman's voice was respectful but far from servile.

"And all night?"

"Oh, yes, sir, of course."

"Why of course?"

"Because," Mrs. Merivale spoke patiently, as if to a dull child, "if she was in all evening she would scarcely go out later, sir."

"You are her caretaker?"

"I have been her nurse ever since she was born. I am now her housekeeper and I take all care of her."

There was something fine about Mrs. Merivale. She gave an impression of one who was tolerating the inquiries of a lot of zanies who must be humoured because they represented the law.

"You live in an island home?"

"Yes." Alma took up the answering again, seeing no reason why Mrs. Merivale should be her spokesman save by way of corroboration.

Then Hart asked the same questions he had asked her before, as to her relations with her uncle, her expectations at his death, and to all the girl replied with a gentle, demure manner that won the admiration and respect of all present.

At last Hart said, plainly:

"I regret the necessity of this, Miss Remsen, but it must be said. You are the one to benefit by the decease of your uncle."

"Yes," she looked at him steadily, with no sign of fear, but again I detected that slight quiver of her eyelid, and wondered what it portended.

"You would have opportunity to reach his room."

"Opportunity?" she looked a little bewildered, and I noticed the lines around the firm set lips of Mrs. Merivale grow even tenser.

"Yes, you possess a latchkey to this house."

"Oh, that!" Alma smiled and I felt sure it was a smile of relief. "Yes, I have always had a latchkey. My uncle gave it to me."

"When?"

"Oh, years ago. When I lived here. Then when I went to live on the island he bade me keep it so I could come over whenever I chose and let myself in."

"Yes. That gave you what we call opportunity."

"And my desire to inherit his estate gave me motive!" she wasn't quite smiling, but nearly. "Well, Mr. Coroner, that may be true, but I didn't come over here with my latchkey and kill my uncle and trick out his bed with flowers. The motive was not strong enough and the opportunity was negligible. I hope you can find my uncle's murderer, but it was not I."

There was something in her simple plain speech that carried conviction. Had I been one of those jurymen I could not have helped believing in the sincerity of that clear, sweet young voice that rang true in its every cadence.

"Then, Miss Remsen, you know nothing of the missing waistcoats?"

"Missing waistcoats?" she repeated, and now I saw that eyelid quiver pitifully.

"Yes, don't repeat my words to gain time. Where are those two waistcoats that disappeared the night your uncle was killed?"

"I haven't the slightest idea."

"Then I will tell you. They have been found, and they were found under a settee in your boathouse——"

"My boathouse!"

"Yes. And wrapped up in them was the Totem Pole that vanished that same night."

Mrs. Merivale's hand shot out and clasped the girl's trembling fingers.

"It is a plant!" she said, "a deep-laid plot to incriminate this innocent child!"

CHAPTER VIII

ALMA'S STATEMENTS

"That is a possible explanation," Hart conceded. "But who would do such a thing? Who would hide those ridiculous properties in that strange place, and why?"

"No, it is not a plant," Alma Remsen said, speaking slowly and seeming to choose her words carefully. "I left the waistcoats in the boathouse myself, when I carried them home day before yesterday."

"Why did you take them home?" Hart spoke gravely but not unkindly.

"My uncle gave them to me."

"Gave them to you! What for?"

"I am making a patchwork quilt, and he told me these two waistcoats were worn and I could have them to cut up for patches. As they were of fine quality silk, I was glad to get them."

I looked at the girl in admiration. She was quite composed, even smiling a little, and she favoured Hart with a glance of confidence, as if sure he would believe her.

"And the Totem Pole?"

"Uncle gave me that, too. He possessed several, and he often gave me little presents like that."

She was quite at ease now, and her eyelids were as steady as the rest of her face and demeanour.

"You were here Tuesday afternoon, then?"

"Yes, between three and four."

"You saw your uncle?"

"Yes, of course."

Something about her manner was disconcerting. At least, it bothered the already harassed Coroner.

I was watching Alma Remsen closely, and it seemed to me she purposely tried to put the Coroner in wrong. There was no overt act or word, but her little glance of surprise or her glimmer of a smile made him seem blundering and inept, and I decided she had such intentions.

This did not lower her in my estimation; indeed, I was fast reaching a point where nothing could disparage her to me. It was not alone her beauty, though she looked fair and sweet to-day, but I was bowled over by her air of courage and determination.

That she had something to conceal, I was positive.

I knew she had been at Pleasure Dome the night of her uncle's death, I knew she denied it. Fatuously I told myself she had her own good reasons for telling a falsehood, and I preferred to believe she was shielding another rather than herself.

Hart was proceeding.

"Were you alone with him?"

Alma's pretty brows contracted in her effort to recollect.

"Most of the time," she said, with the air of humouring an over-inquisitive child. "Mr. Everett was in and out of the room, and Mr. Dean, too, I think."

"Where were you?"

"In my uncle's sitting room in his own suite."

"And then he gave you the silk waistcoats?"

"Yes."

"Which are, you say, worn?"

"Y-yes." There was a slight hesitation this time.

"But Griscom has stated they were nearly new. Why should he give them to you?"

Alma's brows rose in distinct annoyance.

"The question of wear in such a garment is not a matter of fact, it is a matter of opinion. It may be that my uncle considered them more worn than Griscom did, or it may be that, since I admired them, my uncle was willing to part with them, even if they were nearly new. The fact remains, he gave them to me, for the purpose I have told you, and I cannot see what bearing it has on the matter of his death. He also gave me the Totem Pole, and I carried the things home, and inadvertently left them in the boathouse."

Well, if that girl was a liar, she certainly was the cleverest one I had ever seen, and I didn't for a minute believe she was lying.

I glanced at Keeley Moore, but nobody could read his inscrutable face.

I turned my attention to the jury.

Their interested countenances left no doubt of their sympathy with the witness and their readiness to accept her statements.

And apparently Hart himself believed in her. The explanation of the waistcoats was plausible enough. Doubtless, those rich men did give up their clothing before it was worn threadbare, especially if a pretty niece asked for it. And the Totem Pole, too. It was known that Sampson Tracy had been devoted to his niece, although they no longer lived in the same house, and for him to make her presents was far from unbelievable.

And, of course, I believed her.

Even if she had come to Pleasure Dome in the dead of night, that had nothing to do with the waistcoats, which, doubtless, were given to her exactly when and why she had stated.

Yet the girl seemed a mystery.

Coroner Hart contemplated her with a perplexed stare, which she in no way resented.

"Can I tell you anything more?" she asked, helpfully.

Then he glared at her.

"Not now, Miss Remsen," he said, with a new note in his voice. It sounded almost menacing and Merry seemed to spring to attention. "I shall adjourn the inquest, as it was intended merely for identification purposes, and I must look into the case further before I can carry on properly. I will call at your house to-day, and investigate a few things."

"Indeed, you'll do nothing of the sort!", Mrs. Merivale exclaimed, her eyes fairly snapping. They were dark, deep-set eyes, and her gray hair, in wisps round her thin gaunt face, shook with the intensity of her anger. "I'll not have my lamb pestered by such nonsense! Ask her what you like now, and have done with it. But don't come snooping about her home, for you won't be let in!"

Alma quietly turned to the irate woman, and gave her a tender smile.

Then she said to Hart, quietly:

"Mrs. Merivale means no disrespect. She is ignorant of the workings of the law, and is quick to resent what she thinks an intrusion on my privacy. Keep still, Merry. The law must take its course."

More, I felt certain, in response to a caressing touch on her shoulder than by Alma's words, the woman subsided, muttering to herself, but saying nothing audible.

"It must, Miss Remsen," Hart agreed. "I shall therefore call on you to-day, as well as on several other of the witnesses, and I adjourn this inquest for a week."

Now it was Katherine Dallas's turn to look apprehensive.

"I shall not be here," she volunteered. "I am going away for a trip——"

"Not just at present, Mrs. Dallas," the Coroner said, sternly. I was surprised to note how much more master of himself he was when talking to this woman than when he addressed Alma. Yet, surely, the haughty and dignified widow was more awe-inspiring than the gentle girl.

Somehow, everybody seemed disturbed.

Harper Ames looked positively disgruntled. Both secretaries sat, with eyes cast down, as if dismayed at the way things were going. Clearly, there was disappointment that the matter could not be finished up then and there, one way or another.

I came to the conclusion that the Coroner was largely at fault.

Apparently he knew little about conducting an inquest, and though he made no basic errors, he was distinctly floundering and decidedly out of his depth.

"There is much yet to be learned," he announced, and we all, I am sure, silently agreed with him. "There are strange happenings to be explained, stories to be investigated, clues to be traced, evidence to be sifted, and until these things are done the jury cannot come to a decision. As they have seen and identified the deceased man, and have heard the detail of the finding of the body, the funeral may be held and the estate may be administered. But no witness may leave town, and all present must attend the resumed inquest one week from to-day."

Again I looked at the principals. As I could take no part in the conversation, I contented myself with trying to read faces.

Nor was it difficult to do so.

Alma was trembling. Not only did her eyelids quiver, but she shook all over, though quite evidently trying to control herself. Merivale stood at her side; we had all risen now, and the girl leaned heavily upon the arm of the faithful nurse.

Katherine Dallas looked daggers at everybody. Whatever her reason, whatever her mental attitude, she appeared angry at the whole world and inclined to show it.

Ames maintained his usual aspect, which was that of grumpiness.

That is the only word that really describes that man. He was not actively angry, not exactly morose, but just grumpy, and it seemed to be his normal state.

He looked loweringly at the Coroner, at Mrs. Dallas and at Alma. But none of them called forth a varying expression to his grumpy face.

The audience began to disperse, and Ames came directly to Keeley Moore.

"Are you going to take this case?" he asked, in a threatening rather than an urgent manner.

Moore looked at him. Knowing Kee as I did, I could read his thoughts pretty well, and I realized that he was torn between his great desire to investigate this intriguing problem and his disinclination to do it at Ames's behest.

Yet he couldn't ignore Harper Ames and take up the case on his own.

"Yes," he said, deciding quickly, "yes, Mr. Ames, I am most desirous of doing so."

"Then, go ahead, in your own way," and for almost the first

time, I saw Harper Ames look pleased. "Conduct it as you like, and report to me at your convenience."

"I understand, then," Moore said, looking at him closely, "I am to have carte blanche in my manner of procedure, and I am to pursue my investigations no matter in what direction they may lead me?"

I saw a quick spasm of fear flash into Ames's eyes, but it vanished as quickly, and he said, suavely:

"Yes, Mr. Moore. Stop at nothing to get at the truth."

He's the villain, I told myself. He is so sure of his diabolical cleverness, that he thinks he has left no clue and has completely covered his tracks! God help him, when Keeley Moore gets on his trail!

We went into Mr. Tracy's office, a pleasant room off the library.

There were three fine desks, Tracy's own, and those of the secretaries.

Moore had told me to come along, and as Ames made no objection, I did so. The three of us, behind closed doors, ran over the salient details.

"I can offer no sort of explanation of the absurd decorations on the bed," Ames said, "that is your province."

He spoke in a quick, jerky way, as if anxious to delegate the whole matter to Moore and be rid of it once for all.

"Once get the main issues of the affair, and those things will explain themselves," Keeley said, nonchalantly. "Whom do you suspect, Mr. Ames?"

Harper Ames gave a start, and looked up as if he had not heard aright.

"Suspect? I? Oh, nobody. I can't conceive of a human being brutal enough to commit this crime as it was committed. But somebody did, and so, I hope you can bring about his arrest and conviction. Spare no expense——"

"This is not going to be an expensive case, Mr. Ames," Moore told him. "It must be solved by clever work, not by buying up evidence. I admit that sounds rather boastful on my part, but I confess that I am taking up the matter principally because of its unusual features and its bizarre elements. I mean to do my best, and while I shall rely on having your help when and where it may be available, yet I think the most of my work will be done by myself alone."

Again Harper Ames showed that strange gleam of fear in his eyes, but now I thought he feared for some one other than himself. Was he shielding some one? I knew evidence was often misleading because of the desire of some one to protect some one else. But so far, there was not enough evidence even to predicate this.

"Very well," Ames continued. "Work on your own lines. Be as expeditious as possible, but omit no effort. By the terms of Mr. Tracy's will, I shall be in a position to compensate you for your time, and your bill will be paid whether you succeed or not."

"And you have no hint to offer? No advice as to which way to look?"

"I have not. I will only say, it seems to me quite possible that the killing of Mr. Tracy and the strange business of the flowers and oranges may not be the work of the same hand."

"That has occurred to me, too," Kee said. "Now, I don't want to seem insistent, but do tell me your opinion as to the servants."

"I'm not sure." Ames seemed thoughtful. "I can't suspect any wrong of Griscom; he's a faithful old soul, yet he does want his money. Little home on a farm and all that. If he is mixed up in this thing, look out for Bray. She is infatuated with Griscom——"

"And he with her?"

"That I don't know. And it may be only my imagination. The cook is too stupid to do anything really wrong. She has no thought save for her kitchen and household. The other servants I don't know very well. Find out for yourself."

"I shall," and Kee smiled. "Don't think I expect you to hire a dog and then do your own barking. As to the secretaries?"

Though he said this with a most casual air, I knew Moore was listening intently for the reply.

"As to that I can say nothing at all," Ames returned, gravely. "I wouldn't say a word that might inculpate an innocent man. Nor do I say that I think them other than innocent. But you must look it all up, you must weigh and sift and decide for yourself."

"Yes," and Kee nodded his head, "that's what detectives are for."

"Then go to it. Of course, you are free of this house. Any other place you wish to go, you must get permission for yourself. Try to be as expeditious as possible."

I had warmed to Ames. He seemed more of our own sort than I had thought him. But as he rose, thus tacitly dismissing us, his grumpiness returned, and he made a pettish gesture of annoyance at the whole situation.

"Rotten thing to happen!" he exclaimed. "Just now, too, when there were so many crises pending."

"I think I ought to know of those crises, Mr. Ames," Moore said, decidedly.

"Oh, nothing that you don't already know," Ames pulled

himself up. But I was sure that this time he was not strictly truthful. "Only Mr. Tracy's approaching marriage and——"

"Yes, and?"

"Nothing, save some financial matters that are in the lawyers' hands."

Ames was suave again, and I realized that his little burst of anger had been impulsive and was now regretted.

So we left him, and Moore said, as he bowed us out, that we would take a look round Mr. Tracy's apartments upstairs.

"Not just now," Ames said. "They are about to take the body away."

"That won't matter. We won't incommode them," and grasping my arm, Moore fairly hustled me along with him toward the staircase.

We went up to the wing containing the luxurious suite of the dead man.

Looking at it more critically than before, I was delighted with its beautiful furnishings and appointments. We paused in the sitting room, for the undertaker's men were in the bedroom.

Moore began to scrutinize the room. He did not get down on his hands and knees, and show the accepted detective demeanour of "a hound on the scent." But he went about the room with his quick eyes darting here and there for possible indication of an intruder.

The usual appurtenances of the master's occupancy he left apparently unnoticed, but he examined the door sill and the window sills.

The windows, there were two large ones, gave on the lake, or rather, on that dark pool-like stretch of water called the Sunless Sea.

"Come and look out here, Norris," he said. "Can you imagine any one jumping or diving into that bottomless pit?"

"Yes," I returned, "I can easily imagine it. But he would have to be a master diver and a master swimmer. Also, a fearless man and a desperate one."

"Well put, old chap. Clearly and succinctly, I'll say. He would, indeed, have to be all those things. And he was about five feet eight inches tall, and not a heavy weight, and he wore white flannels and tennis shoes and carried in his hand something painted red."

"Marvellous, Holmes, marvellous!" I managed to ejaculate, though I was nearly struck dumb at his speech. "Now, I won't be your Watson, unless you tell me how you picked up, or made up, all that."

"Of course, I'll tell you. You well know I'm not the sort of mutt that likes to be mysterious. And, too, I want your corroboration. First, you see the print on the white painted window sill of what can

70

only be the rubber sole of a tennis shoe. You see there's by no means a full foot-print, but there is enough to show the nubbly sole."

He was right. I could discern clearly, though faintly, a few of the imprints undeniably made by a sole of a tennis shoe.

"Not enough to tell whether the wearer of the shoe had his foot turned in toward the room or outward," I offered.

"No," he returned, eying me sharply, "but the law of probabilities makes me believe it is turned outward. It is hard to think of the murderer poising himself on the sill and diving into that black water, but far harder to visualize him coming in by such an entrance!"

"Go on," I said, a bit crossly, for I didn't at all like it.

"Our friend, the murderer, was about five feet eight, because I am five feet ten and a half, and here at the sides of the window frame, we see two sets of fingerprints, faint again, but there, and they are at a height of two and a half inches below where mine would strike if I took hold to pull myself up to the window sill."

"You can't get anything from those prints," I told him. "They're too faint. A mere hint only."

"I only need a mere hint. And anyway, I'm only proving the exit of our criminal by this window, and so down into the lake."

"And his clothes!" I jeered. "A straw hat, did you say?"

"I did not. I said white flannels, because here's a shred of such caught in a splinter of the upright of the window frame."

"I refuse to believe in 'shreds of cloth clenched in the victim's hand.'"

"Not a shred, really, just a thread, a strand, but it's to the zealous, confirmation strong! And, note that he carried something painted red in his right hand. See the mark, just above his right hand-print, that is indubitably made by a piece of painted wood."

"The devil it is! I say, Moore, you're going dotty over this thing. At any rate, don't give it all to Hart or March, for they'll make ducks and drakes of it in short order."

"No, I shall give it to nobody. I shall use it all myself. I only show it to you, because I want you to witness it. This evidence may be removed, and I want you to swear it was here."

"I can't swear those are fingerprints," I complained. "They're too faint. You can't swear to that yourself."

"I'll get the fingerprint man up here, or get his outfit. It's a wonder what they can do with the merest smudges. And, I say, Norry, what's the trouble? Don't you want me to find clues? Don't you want me to unearth the villain? You didn't murder Tracy, did you?"

"No, but do go slowly, Kee. You're so impulsive, so headstrong.

Now, that red streak, a mere blur, may have been here for days—even weeks."

"Not in this house. Do you see any other smudges or smears on this immaculate white paint? Enamel paint, of the finest sort. Every fingerprint is wiped off within twenty-four hours, I'm sure. That's why I want to be sure of these."

The men were gone now, so we stepped into the bedroom.

Save that the master was absent, the room was much as we had already seen it. The flowers, now withered, still lay on the pillows, and the crackers and orange were on the floor where Doctor Rogers had flung them.

The feather duster seemed not to interest Kee, but he scrutinized the window sill with care.

"No signs here, you see. And, too, there's a balcony. It would be easier to dive from the sitting-room window. So that's what our friend did. See, here's the lady's scarf. Now learn, my boy, to distinguish between important and non-important clues. Without doubt, the sentimental Sampson kept that scarf by him as a reminder and souvenir of his bride to be. Most likely, he went to bed, carrying it with him. Perhaps wrapped it about him, or held it to his cheek."

"Don't be silly!"

"Not silly at all. I see you know nothing of fetish worship, remnants of which survive among us moderns in the form of just such souvenirs. So, I deduce the murderer had no hand in providing the scarf. But the flowers had to be brought from their vases, the crackers and fruit from the table, the duster from its proper abiding place, all these things were achieved by our tennis-soled friend."

"And the nail?" I snapped at him.

"Yes," he said, "and the nail."

CHAPTER IX

CLUES

"And what was the nail driven home with?" I pursued, looking about.

"That's a queer thing, too," he returned. "Some heavy mallet or hammer must have been used. True, it could have been driven by some other hard or heavy object, but I see nothing indicative about. No bronze book-ends or iron doorstop."

We scanned the room, but saw no implement that would act as a hammer.

"I think I may say," Keeley went on, "that never have I seen a case with so many bizarre points. To be sure they may be all faked in an attempt to bewilder and mislead the investigators, but even so, such a number of clues, whether real or spurious, ought to lead somewhere."

"They will," I assured him. "Where are you going to begin?"

"I don't know where I shall begin, but I shall end up with the watch in the water pitcher. That, you will find, will be the bright star in this galaxy of clues."

"Just as a favour, Kee, do tell me why you stress that so. Why is that silly act more illuminating than the other queernesses?"

"No, Gray, I won't tell you that now. Not that I want to be mysterious, but that may be my trump card, and I don't want to expose it prematurely. You'd know yourself if you'd ever studied medical works."

"Medical works! I can't see any therapeutic value in the incident. Is it voodoo, or a medicine-man stunt?"

Griscom came into the room just then, and Moore asked him again as to the watch.

But we gained no new knowledge. The watch had been lying on a small jewel tray on the dresser. The water pitcher had been on a near-by table. It seemed, like all the rest of the inexplicable circumstances, a mere bit of wanton mischief.

"Why do you look so worried, Griscom?" Kee said, eying the man closely.

"I am worried, sir. About them weskits."

"Oh, pshaw, they're of small consequence compared to the graver questions we have to face."

"Yes, sir, but it's queer. Now, I know those two weskits were in

73

their right place Wednesday morning. And Miss Alma said the master gave 'em to her of a Tuesday afternoon."

"Oh, she just mistook the day," I said, hastily, anxious to keep her name out of the discussion.

But Moore was interested at once.

"Are you sure?" he asked.

"Perfectly sure," the man replied. "Miss Alma was here Tuesday afternoon and the master may have given her the weskits then, but she didn't carry them home, for they were here Wednesday morning."

"One of you must be mistaken as to the day," I repeated. "And it doesn't matter, anyway."

"Oh, keep still, Gray," Kee said, impatiently. "What about the Totem Pole, Griscom? Was that here Wednesday morning?"

"I don't know for certain——" He looked perplexed.

"Of course you don't," I broke in, irrepressibly. "You can't remember exactly incidents that made no real impression on you at the time. Nobody can. And don't try to be positive about these things when you've really only a vague recollection."

"No, sir," Griscom said, speaking deferentially enough, but I caught a slight gleam of obstinacy in his eye.

"Are you talking about those waistcoats?" asked Everett, coming into the room.

"Yes," Kee said, "why?"

"Only that I'm puzzled. Miss Remsen says her uncle gave them to her on Tuesday, but I know that he wore the dark blue moire one on Wednesday."

"At dinner time?" Moore asked.

"Yes, we don't dress in summer, unless there are ladies here. He had it on at dinner I'm positive."

"Then it's all part of the planted evidence," I informed them. "Whoever staged all the foolish scene on the bed, also grabbed up two waistcoats and the Totem Pole, made a bundle of them and deposited it in Miss Remsen's boathouse."

"Then why did she say she wanted them for patchwork——"

"She didn't at first," I urged, not realizing where my argument led. "But she was so put about and bewildered by that fool coroner that she scarcely knew what she was saying——"

"I think you scarcely know what you're saying, Gray," and Moore looked at me in kindly admonition. "You'd better hush up, if you don't mind. I'm not sure Miss Remsen needs an advocate, but if she does, your incoherent babblings won't do her any good."

Though he smiled, his tone was serious, and I began to see I was making a fool of myself.

I turned on my heel and left the room, not trusting myself to hush up to the degree desired. In the sitting room, I saw Billy Dean, looking disconsolate.

I was surprised, for he had seemed cheerful enough up to now.

On a sudden impulse, and with a glance that he could not mistake for other than confidential, I said:

"So you saw the canoe Wednesday night?"

"Yes," he said, answering my eyes rather than my words. Then realizing his slip, he said, quickly, "No, not a canoe, I heard a motor boat about midnight."

"Yes, and a canoe later," I persisted. "Look out, Dean, I'm not investigating, I'm only anxious to help—the innocent," I finished, a little lamely.

"I don't get you," the young man said, stubbornly, and again the red flamed in his cheeks.

"Oh, yes, you do, and please understand we're at one in this matter. I want you to promise not to say anything about it to any one. You see, your unfortunate trick of blushing like a schoolgirl gives you away, and makes you seem to admit far more than you know. Now, before Detective March or Keeley Moore gets after you, just you tell me what you know and let me advise you. I'm as loyal to Miss Remsen as you can possibly be, even if you are in love with her and I'm not."

I made this not entirely veracious statement to set the poor chap's mind at rest, for I could see dawning jealousy in his frank and open countenance.

He responded to my sincerity of manner and tone, and speaking almost in a whisper, said:

"I didn't see her, my room is in the other wing, but I heard Alma's paddling. I'd know her stroke among a thousand. Nobody paddles as she does."

"Oh, you couldn't recognize a mere paddle stroke!"

"Yes, I could. It's unique, I tell you. She has a peculiar rhythm, and if you know it, it's unmistakable."

"At what time was this?"

"About half past one; a few minutes later, just after the clock in the hall had chimed the half hour."

"Why do you tell me this?"

He glared at me. "That's a nice question, when you've fairly dragged it out of me! But I'm banking on your statement that you're loyal to Alma and I'm hoping that you can somehow ward off inquiries from Mr. Moore or keep the police away from her house."

"You don't think she had anything to do with——"

"Of course, I know Alma Remsen had nothing to do with her

75

uncle's death, if that's what you're trying to say, but I do believe she was here late that night, and if that fact is discovered, it means trouble all round."

He had suddenly acquired a dignity quite at variance with his former boyish embarrassment, and spoke earnestly and steadily.

"Why would she come here at such an hour?"

"She—she comes at any time—she has her own key——" He was floundering again.

"Yes, I know, but at half past one at night! What could be the explanation?"

"I can't tell you——I daren't tell you," he moaned like a child. "But oh, Mr. Norris, do stand by! Do use any tact or cleverness you may possess to keep the hounds off her track! She will be persecuted, unless we can save her!" He began to look wild-eyed, and I began to fear that Miss Remsen had even a worse and more imbecile helper in him than in me.

But the whole affair was growing in interest, and I was glad to have a sympathizer in my belief in Alma Remsen's innocence, whatever sort he might be.

For I had caught a few words from the next room and I felt certain that Everett and Keeley Moore were talking over the strange story of Alma and the waistcoats.

Feeling I could do no more with Dean just then, I went back to the bedroom.

"Sifting clues?" I asked, trying to speak casually.

Kee looked at me, and smiled a little.

"Absent clues rather than present ones," he said. "You see, the waistcoats and the Totem Pole disappeared, but so did the plate—the fruit plate."

"Is that important?" I asked.

"Why, yes, in a way. Everything that is here or that isn't here is important."

"A bit cryptic, but I grasp your meaning," I told him. "Then the hammer that belongs to the nail is important?"

"Very much so," Kee answered, gravely. "Do you know where it is?"

"I don't, but it seems to me you haven't looked for it very hard. If the murderer is one of this household, presumably he used a hammer belonging here."

"Then it loses its importance. The hammer is only of interest if it was brought in from outside."

"Have you made any headway at all, Kee?"

"Not much, I confess. Mr. Everett here inclines to Ames——"

"And Ames inclines to Everett," was the somewhat surprising observation of the secretary himself.

"Yes," he went on, as I looked at him in amazement, "but I think, I hope, Ames only suspects me because it's the conventional thing to do. In stories, you know, nine tenths of the crimes are committed by the confidential secretary."

"Not so many," I said, judicially: "Four tenths, at most. Then, three tenths by the butler, three tenths by the inheriting nephew, and two tenths by——"

"Hold up, Gray," Keeley cried, "you've used up your quota of tenths already. But Ames is a really fine suspect."

"Except that he can't dive and I can," Everett helped along. "And there's no way out of this locked apartment except through a window. And all the windows are on the Sunless Sea."

"Could you dive into that and come up smiling?" asked Kee.

"I could," Everett said, "but I'd rather not. I know the rocks and all that, but it's a tricky stunt. Ames could never do it."

"Unless he's been hoaxing you all as to his prowess in the water," Moore suggested.

"Yes, that might be," Everett assented, thoughtfully.

Then Moore and I started for home. As we left the house, he proposed we go in a boat, of which there seemed to be plenty and to spare at the dock.

In preference to a canoe, Keeley selected a trim round-bottomed rowboat, and we started off.

He did the rowing, by choice, and he bent to his oars in silence. I too felt disinclined to talk, and we shot along the water, propelled by his long steady strokes.

I looked about me. The whole scene was a setting for peace and happiness—not for crime. Yet here was black crime, stalking through the landscape, aiming for Pleasure Dome, and clutching in its wicked hand the master of the noble estate.

I looked back at the wonderful view. The great house, built on a gently sloping hill, shone white in the summer sunlight. The densely growing trees, judiciously thinned out or cut into vistas, made a perfect background, and the foreground lake, shimmering now as the sun caught its wavelets, veiled its dangers and treachery beneath a guise of smiling light.

We went on and on and I suddenly realized that we had passed the Moore bungalow.

"Keeley," I said, thinking he had forgotten to land, "where are you going?"

"To the Island," he replied, and his face wore an inscrutable look, "Come along, Gray, but for Heaven's sake don't say anything

77

foolish. Better not open your mouth at all. Better yet, stay in the boat——"

"No," I cried, "I'm going with you. Don't be silly, Kee, I sha'n't make a fool of myself."

"Well, try not to, anyway," he said, grimly, and then we made a landing at Alma Remsen's home.

It was a tidy little dock and trim boathouse that received us, and I realized the aptness of the name "Whistling Reeds."

For the tall reeds that lined some stretches of its shore were even now whistling faintly in the summer breeze. A stronger wind would indeed make them voiceful.

Back of the reeds were trees, and I had a passing thought that never had I seen so many trees on one island. So dense that they seemed like an impenetrable growth, the path cut through them to the house was not at once discernible.

"This way," Kee said, and struck into a sort of lane between the sentinel poplars and hemlocks.

But a short walk brought us out into a great clearing where was a charming cottage and most pleasant grounds and gardens.

There were terraces, flower beds, tennis court, bowling green and a field showing a huge target, set up for archery practice.

It fascinated me, and I no longer wondered that Miss Remsen loved her island home. The house itself, though called a cottage, was a good-sized affair, of two and a half stories, with verandahs and balconies, and a hospitable atmosphere seemed to pervade the porches, furnished with wicker chairs and chintz cushions.

Yet the place was so still, so uninhabited looking that I shuddered involuntarily. I became conscious of a sinister effect, an undercurrent of something eerie and strange.

I glanced off at the trees and shrubbery. It was easily seen that the Island, of two or three acres, I thought, was bright and cheerful only immediately around the house. Surrounding the clearing for that, the trees closed in, and the result was like an enormous, lofty wall of impenetrable black woods.

I quickly came back to the house, and as we went up the steps, Alma Remsen came out on the porch.

I shall never forget how she looked then.

For the first time I saw her close by without a hat. Her hair, of golden brown, but bright gold in the sunlight, was in soft short ringlets like a baby's curls. I know a lot, having sisters, about marcel and permanent, about water waves and finger curls, but this hair, I recognized, had that unusual attribute, longed for by all women: it was naturally curly.

The tendrils clustered at the nape of her neck and broke into

78

soft, thick curls at the top of her head. I had never seen such fascinating hair, and dimly wondered what it was like before she had it cut short.

She wore a sort of sports suit of white silk with bands of green.

She glanced down at this apologetically.

"I ought to be in black," she said, "or, at least, all white. But I am, when I go over to the mainland. Here at home, it doesn't seem to matter. Does it?"

She looked up at me appealingly, though with no trace of coyness.

"Of course not," I assured her. "Our affection is not made or marred by the colour of a garment."

This sounded a bit stilted, even to me, but Kee had told me not to make a fool of myself and I was trying hard to obey.

"Sit down," she said, hospitably, but though calm, she was far from being at ease.

"We're only going to stay a minute," Kee said. "We must get home to luncheon. It's late now, and my wife will be furious. Miss Remsen, I think I'll speak right out and not beat about the bush."

She turned rather white, but sat listening, her hands clasped in her lap and her little white-shod foot tapping nervously on the porch floor.

"I want to ask you," Keeley Moore spoke in a tone of such kindness that I could see Alma pluck up heart a bit, "about the waistcoats. Though it may be a trifling matter, yet great issues may hang on it. When you said your uncle gave them to you, were you strictly truthful?"

She sat silent, looking from one to the other of us. When she glanced at me I was startled at the message in her eyes. If ever a call of SOS was signalled, it was then. Without a word or a gesture her gaze implored my help.

But with all the willingness in the world, what could I do? Keeley had warned me against making a fool of myself, and though I would gladly have defied him to serve her, I could see no way to do so, fool or no fool. All I could do, was to give her back gaze for gaze and try to put in my eyes all the sympathy and help that were surging up in my heart.

I think she understood, and yet I could see a shadow of disappointment that I could, as she saw, do nothing definite.

Moore was waiting for his answer, but she was deliberate of manner and speech.

"By what right are you questioning me, Mr. Moore?" she said.

"Principally by right of my interest in you and your welfare and

79

my great desire to be of service to you." Kee's sincerity was beyond all doubt.

"That is the truth?"

"Yes, Miss Remsen, that is the truth."

"Then, I will tell you, that you can be of service to me only by refraining from questioning me and ceasing to interest yourself in my welfare."

The asperity of the words was contradicted by the supplicating glance and the troubled face of the girl before us. Her eyelids quivered with that agonized trembling I had learned to know, and she fairly bit her lips in an effort to preserve her poise.

"I'm sorry not to take you at your word, and leave you at once, but I must warn you that the police will doubtless come to see you, and I'm sure you are in need of advice."

"Police!" she breathed, scarcely audibly.

"Yes; Not Hart, but more likely Detective March. He is not an unkind man, but he will do his duty, and it will be an ordeal for you. Now, won't you let me help you, as a friend, or, if not, won't you call a lawyer, of good standing and repute?"

"A lawyer!" she breathed, exactly as she had spoken of the police. Clearly, the poor child was at her wits' end. The reason for her distress I did not see, for surely nobody could dream of her being mixed up in a crime. The obvious explanation was that she was shielding somebody, and this was my theory.

I came to a swift conclusion that she had gone to Pleasure Dome that night, that she had seen or heard the murderer at his fell deed, and that it had so unnerved her that she could not control herself when thinking of it.

This seemed to point to Billy Dean, that is, if she cared for him as he did for her.

Kee was forging ahead.

"Yes. Please try to realize, Miss Remsen, that the visit from the police detective is inevitable. He will doubtless come this afternoon. You will have to see him; one can't evade the law. Now, let me help you to be a little prepared for him, and not let him throw you into spasms of terrified silence, or, worse, impetuous and incriminating statements."

Still looking at him steadily, Alma Remsen seemed to change. Her face grew calm, even haughty; her lips set in a straight line that betokened determination and courage; and her eyes fairly gleamed with a beautiful bravery that transformed her into a veritable goddess of war.

She seemed to have taken up her sword and her shield, and I

think it was at that moment that I realized that I loved her and adored her as something far above earthly mortals.

I couldn't help her, at least, not at the moment, but I could worship her and did so, with the innermost fibres of my being.

Then this new Alma spoke.

"Mr. Moore," she said, "and Mr. Norris, I thank you for this visit. I thank you for the kindness that prompted it, and for your offers of assistance. But there is nothing you can do, either of you. I am alone in the world; alone, I must fight my battles and conquer my foes. Alone I must defend my actions and accept my misfortunes. I live alone, I shall always be alone, and alone I must decide upon my course in this present crisis. Please believe I am grateful and please believe I am sorry not to accept your kindly offered assistance. But I cannot tell you anything, I cannot—I cannot—Merry!"

Her final despairing call brought the old nurse on the run.

"Yes, lamb, yes, my darling,—there, there——"

Mrs. Merivale clasped the trembling girl to her bosom and glared at us as at vile interlopers.

"Please to go away, gentlemen," she said, in a repressed tone that indicated wrath behind it. "Please leave my young lady for the present. She will see you, if she wishes, at some other time. But now, she is nervous and all wrought up with the horror of her uncle's death. If you are men, let her alone!"

The last plea was brought out with a dramatic touch worthy of a tragedy queen, and I know I felt like a worm of the dust and I devoutly hoped that Keeley felt even more so.

He gave one last bit of unsolicited advice.

"You'd better be with Miss Remsen when the police come, Mrs. Merivale," he said, and no one could have put any construction on his words other than the kindest and most disinterested counsel.

Then we went away, and Keeley rowed us home without a word.

CHAPTER X

DISCUSSION

If Whistling Reeds had seemed desolate and sinister, Variable Winds was just the opposite. Clean, wind-swept, cheerful with flowers and only pleasantly shaded by the waving trees, the place was like sanctuary after the forbidding aspect of the island home.

Luncheon was ready and the two women who awaited our coming were not at all reproachful, but welcomed us with smiles.

"Dust up a bit and then come along," admonished Lora, and we obeyed.

At the table, though the subject of the tragedy was not entirely taboo, there was no real discussion, until we were, later, seated in the lounge, comfortably smoking and resting from our strenuous morning.

"The keynote is the missing waistcoats," Kee announced, oracularly.

"You said the keynote was the watch in the water pitcher," I reminded him.

"They are part of the same note," he informed me. "The work of the same hand and equally illuminating as signboards."

"Oh, if you're going to be mysterious——"

"I'm not, Gray, but I can't announce decisions that are not yet entirely clear in my own mind. I'm sorry Doctor Rogers went away— he could read the message of the watch at once. But I don't want to put it up to any other doctor."

"Well, of course I can't help you, as you are so close-minded—"

"Nonsense, Gray," said Lora, "of course we can help. The watch may or may not be of such great importance, but it surely isn't all there is of it. Nor the waistcoats, either. To me, those things seem merely adjuncts of the rest of the queer performance, the flowers and feather duster and all that."

"But the waistcoats are in contradictory stories," I argued. "Miss Remsen said she took them home Tuesday afternoon, and left them in the boathouse where they were found. Griscom says they were in their place on Wednesday. Then Everett came along and said Mr. Tracy wore one of them, the blue one, Wednesday night at dinner."

"Well, then," and Lora looked at me keenly, "what point are you making, Gray? These stories seem to stultify Miss Remsen's statement."

"I'm making the point," I declared, "that the girl isn't quite responsible for her own statements; she doubtless told her uncle she would like the satin for her patchwork and he probably said she could have it. But she didn't carry the waistcoats away with her, Tuesday afternoon—that we know. So, what conclusion is there, but that, as the old nurse said, it is all a plant? Somebody came in the night, killed Mr. Tracy, and then, after fixing up all that jiggery-pokery, went off carrying the waistcoats and Totem Pole, and carefully planted them in Alma Remsen's boathouse. I can't see anything incriminating to the girl in all that."

"Gray, dearie," Lora said, with a queer, affectionate little smile, "you couldn't see anything incriminating to Miss Remsen with a Lick telescope! Now, that's all right, and I'm not cavilling, but unless you can approach this matter with an unbiassed mind, maybe you'd better keep out of it."

"Keep out of it nothing!" I exclaimed. "I admit I admire Miss Remsen, but that's all the more reason to see things clearly and stay in the discussion."

"Right!" said Maud, "and I vote that Gray be in it all, and that we pay especial attention to his opinions."

I looked at her quickly, to see if she was guying me, but she was not, and I at once recovered my balance, my self-respect and an added cocksure air that caused the Moores, both of them, great amusement.

But I was not at all daunted by their smiles and I went on.

"My opinion is this," I stated, "the man who killed Sampson Tracy is as clever as they come. He fixed up all the rubbishy evidence to mislead the investigators. But, perhaps on purpose, perhaps accidentally, he led directly to Miss Remsen in the matter of the waistcoats and the Totem Pole. And so——"

"Now, Graysie, dear," and Kee threw the stub of his cigar into the ash tray, "I'm ready to talk. So, call a halt on the waistcoat-totem matter, and let's get down to cases."

"It's a case, all right," said Lora, whose fine eyes were gazing directly at her husband, as she concentrated on the subject. "Kee, you've got your chance!"

"Chance!" Moore echoed. "I'm no Sherlock, I'm ready to say right out that I'm all afloat, absolutely at sea, in this thing."

Somehow this comforted me. I feared he would jump at once to a conclusion that somehow incriminated Alma Remsen, and I was greatly relieved that he didn't.

Wanting to be helpful, I volunteered: "How about the weapon? There's the nail, of course, but what about the hammer or mallet? I can't see that nail driven without a heavy implement."

Kee looked at me.

"No," he said, "I can't either. How about a croquet mallet?"

"That would fit," I responded. "Know of any here-abouts?"

"Not precisely. But the tennis court at Whistling Reeds used to be a croquet ground."

I quailed, but I hoped I didn't show it.

"And that proves?" I said, jauntily.

"Nothing but possibility."

"Which isn't much."

"No, it isn't much." Kee looked harassed. "But a lot of little bits of evidence, added together, make a——"

"Make a muckle," I jibed. "All right, what's your muckle?"

"That Alma Remsen knows more about this matter than she's telling."

Moore's deadly still tone, more than his words, struck a chill of terror to my heart.

For a moment, knowing his great wisdom as well as I did, I was tempted to tell him everything, but caution held me back, and I only said, "it may be."

Lora looked at me, curiously.

"Gray," she said, "you don't know anything, do you?" I was glad she put it like this.

"No, Lora," I replied, "I don't know anything. If I did, I'd speak out. But I do believe that there is a deep, dark, underlying mystery that none of us understands, and I wish I could see into it."

"Kee will see into it," she said, confidently, and I could only respond: "I hope to Heaven he will."

Kee sat without speaking for a moment or two, and then said:

"Gray, what was the reason for Miss Remsen's sudden change of base while we were talking to her?"

"Change of base?" I said, stupidly.

"Yes. Don't be an imbecile. I know you noticed it. It was just after I told her the police would come to interview her. That seemed to spur her or stir her up in some way, for she at once became a different being. More alert and alive, more determined."

"Yes, I noticed it," I told him. "I can't explain it except to say that she was startled at the idea of a police interview, and it brought out her natural bravery and courage. She rose to the occasion and I've no doubt she will meet Hart with proper dignity and poise."

"It won't be Hart, it will be March. March is a good man, but I doubt if he can swing this case."

"Of course he can't," I declared. "But you're going to do the swinging, yourself."

"Then I'd better begin. Now let's marshal our facts. First of all, we have the collection of properties found on the bed. Was that all the work of one hand?"

"Yes," I said, "but not necessarily the hand of the murderer."

"That's right," and Moore nodded assent. "I'm inclined to think a waggish-minded visitor followed up the murderer and arranged that scenery."

"Why?" asked Lora, very thoughtfully.

"I can think of no reason," Kee returned, "except in an effort to direct suspicion away from the real criminal."

"Who would do that?"

"Only a clever and watchful person, determined to shield the murderer."

"Set up a hypothetical case," suggested Maud. "Say, Mrs. Dallas was the murderer——"

"How absurd," cried Lora, "why should she kill the man she expected to marry?"

"That we don't know," Maud went on in her calm way. "But there may have been reasons. Suppose Mr. Tracy had learned some secret in Mrs. Dallas's past——"

"Go on," Kee said, briefly, as Maud looked at him questioningly.

"I know it sounds melodramatic, but the whole affair is melodramatic, and those clues don't seem to lead anywhere. Well, suppose Mrs. Dallas did it—killed him, I mean—and suppose somebody saw her who cared for her, Mr. Ames or Mr. Everett, or—or anybody. Mightn't he trump up all that funny business to make it seem as if she could not have done it?"

"I don't think you've struck it quite right, Maud," Keeley said, "but I will say there's a germ of thought in your theory. Granting two people concerned, there's no reason to think them accomplices, it's far more likely one is covering up the deeds of the other."

"All of which is fantastic and not founded on fact," Lora put in. "It's only imagination, and one can imagine anything."

"You have no use for imagination?" I asked her, smiling.

"Yes, when it is admittedly imagination, as in a fairy story or a romance. But imagination must not be used as a basis for argument."

"She's right," Keeley said, slowly. "Lora's usually right. Now what facts have we, outside the feather-duster lot?"

"The people themselves," I offered. "The relationships between the people and the motives of the people."

"That's more like it," and Kee gave me a glance of approval. "Take the household first. Who's the most likely suspect?"

"Mrs. Dallas," I said, promptly.

"She isn't in the household."

"Same as. She has a latchkey, so that makes her practically one of them."

"Then Alma Remsen is in the same case."

"Same case," I agreed, knowing better than to combat him.

"All right, go on. What's the widow's motive?"

I knew Moore's methods. He liked to have us make suggestions that he could accept or discard, thereby giving his mind something to work on.

"We can't get at her motive," I told him, "because we know too little about her. A personal interview with her is needed, and then she would probably, or at least perhaps, let slip some hint of why she wanted Sampson Tracy out of her way."

"She'd have to hate him," said Maud, doubtfully.

"Whoever killed him must have hated him," Kee declared. "It was a brutal murder——"

"Don't over-stress the brutality," Lora put in. "It was horrible, of course, but to my mind it was less dreadful than shooting or stabbing."

"Where did the murderer get his nail?" mused Kee.

"The nail and the hammer," Lora said, "inclines me to the servants, or the secretaries. I can't see Mrs. Dallas or Alma Remsen coming to the house armed with a hammer and nail! They might bring a pistol or a dagger, but the implement used must have been picked up impulsively or impetuously, in the Tracy pantries or offices."

"Unless the murderer acted on the story Maud told of, the Spanish story of The Nail," I observed.

"Rather far-fetched," Kee returned. "I'd have to see a copy of that book in a suspect's possession before I'd take much stock in that theory."

"I rather fancy it," Maud insisted. "Any of our suspects, and I suppose they include all who were questioned by the coroner, may have read that book."

"The servants?" I asked.

"Yes, often servants read books that they run across, though they'd never dream of buying them."

"Then Griscom for choice," Moore said. "Say his motive is a desire to get his legacy at once. Say his friendship for his master is not so great as he pretends, and there's no question of his opportunity. Say he read that gruesome tale, and concluded it would be a fine way to get his money quickly. Then, after his deed is accomplished, he has imagination enough, or ingenuity enough to fix up all those tricks on the bed, and in his zeal he rather overdid it."

"Your own imagination is running away with you," I declared. "It may all be true, but you've no atom of proof, nor even an atom of evidence against Griscom more than any other servant. Sally Bray-"

"Sally Bray may have been Griscom's accomplice. Isn't she in love with him?"

"Is she?" I inquired. "There's the trouble, Kee, we don't know enough facts. Is Sally in love with the butler? Is Mrs. Dallas in love with the secretary? Is Harper Ames in love with Mrs. Dallas? Get these things settled for certain, and then try to fit in your theories."

"That's so, Gray," Moore agreed. "And I see Mr. Police Detective March coming our way. I hate to acknowledge it, but he may know more, in his ordinary police way, than we hifalutin, transcendent detectives have, so far, been able to ferret out."

I glanced out of the window to see the stolid-looking man tramping along toward our door.

Although he showed little alertness or eagerness, there was a sort of power in the way he carried himself that gave me a feeling of confidence.

He came in as Kee rose to greet him, spoke to the ladies in a preoccupied way, and seated himself comfortably in a big easy chair.

"Well," he said, "I've been to see the Remsen girl."

"What about her?" Kee asked.

"Nothing, so far. She's rattled to death, and all upset, of course, but though I think she's trying to hide something, I'm sure it's nothing of real importance. I mean, she thinks she knows something about somebody that seems to her of evidential value, but it isn't."

"How do you know it isn't?"

"This way, Mr. Moore. She gets embarrassed at the wrong places."

"Go on, say more about it."

"It's hard to explain so as to make it plausible. But when I ask her about her doings that night, or about her relations with her uncle, or her feeling towards Mrs. Dallas, she's as unconcerned and un-self-conscious as a child. But when I refer to those waistcoats or that painted pole, she gets queer-like all in a minute."

"And you gather from that?"

"That she is worried to death about the waistcoats because somebody must have put them in her boathouse to incriminate her, and that scares her. While any talk of the actual murder seems not to disturb her nearly so much."

"You have imagination, Mr. March," Moore said, looking at him with a sort of admiration. "Or you couldn't see all that."

"No, Mr. Moore," the policeman looked earnest, "that's only

seeing things as they are. I saw all that in Miss Remsen's face and attitude. It isn't imagination a detective needs, it's ability to read the facts right. It's the criminal who has to have imagination."

"This present murderer surely had it," Moore said.

"Yes, if he is the one who fixed up the doodads around the dead man. Sometimes I think he was, and then again, I don't see how he could have been."

"Why?"

"Well, the murder, even though a cruel stroke, was the work of an intelligent mind. A less imaginative brain would have chosen shooting or stabbing as a method. But granting a mentality that could think of and carry out a killing like that nail business, I can't reconcile it with a personality that would collect those gewgaws and scatter them around."

"Why wasn't that done with intent to mislead——"

"Oh, mislead, yes. But why so much of it? That's the point. A few flowers, now, even the crucifix—all right. But the exaggeration. The superfluity. The piling on of the orange and crackers, the lady's scarf, the watch in the water pitcher——"

"The missing waistcoats, Totem Pole, and fruit plate," Keeley broke in, as if unable longer to keep still. "What do you make of all these things, March?"

"What I said. Exaggeration, overdoing. So, we must hunt for a nature, a temperament, that is extravagant and over generous, rather than a well-balanced mind."

"Good work," Keeley Moore exclaimed, for he was always ready to acclaim merit, and he thought the detective showed real insight. "And you didn't discover this extravagant spirit in Miss Remsen?"

"Not a bit of it. She's a lovely lady, and she may know something she's keeping quiet about, but she had no hand in the crime. She had no hand in the decoration of the deathbed in that fantastic manner. Motive she had, opportunity she had, but after all they're not everything."

I blessed the man in my heart for this whole-souled acquittal of Alma, and I began to feel more interest in the matter.

"Then, who's your pet suspect?" Kee was asking.

"I have four," the detective answered, frankly. "Mr. Ames, Mrs. Dallas and the two secretaries."

"Quite a net full," Keeley smiled. "Do you care to detail your reasons? Or do you think I ought to do my own investigating?"

"No," said March, ponderously. He was a big man, heavy of voice as of body, and he seemed to weigh his words as he spoke them. "No, Mr. Moore, I'm only too glad to tell you all I know, to give you all I get, for I know you are the one to make the deductions from my facts."

"All right, then, go ahead. Motives first, for all four. What about the will?"

"It will be read to-morrow afternoon, after the funeral. But I will tell you the gist of it. It's really no secret, but better not mention its terms until after they're made public."

Moore nodded, and March went on:

"The bulk of the fortune and estate goes to Miss Remsen, as she is Tracy's only natural heir. There is a gift of fifty thousand dollars to Mrs. Dallas and twenty-five thousand each to the two secretaries. Oh, yes, and fifty thousand dollars to Mr. Ames."

"This still leaves a big fortune for Miss Remsen?" Lora asked.

"Yes, ma'am. Old Tracy had between two and three millions, I'm told. So with the servants' bequests and charities included, that only runs to, say, two or three hundred thousand, and the young lady is left very nicely fixed."

"Servants get much?"

"Griscom, ten thousand, and some stocks besides. Mrs. Fenn about the same. The other servants in proportion, according as to how long they've been employed."

"Well," Keeley mused, "that's enough about the conditions of the will to work on. Now, granting greed as the motive, we have your four suspects and Griscom and the cook all possibly guilty."

"Yes, and you needn't exclude the other servants. I mean they all had equal motive and the same opportunity. But it never was a servant's job. Never."

March looked so positive that Moore asked him to say why.

"No clues," came the answer. "You see, granting some one of the servants had the ingenuity, the imagination, to cook up this way of doing the killing, he would have taken a hammer and nail from the house stores."

"Didn't he?"

"He did not. I've combed over the whole kitchen outfit, pantries, offices, storerooms, cellars, garage and every such place, and I know every nail and hammer in the whole place. And there's no such nail as that one used to end Sampson Tracy's life in the whole layout."

"And the hammer?" Moore looked quizzical.

"I grant the hammer is less easily identifiable. But I've hunted for fingerprints on the hammers and mallets around the premises, and there are no prints on them except the ones legitimately there. This isn't proof positive, but it's fairly so, when you take it in connection with the absence of any such nails as we're searching for, and the unlikelihood of any of the under servants being able to get access to Mr. Tracy's apartments. Except for Griscom, none of them is allowed in the living rooms at night, and I don't suspect Griscom—yet."

"Now Ames and the two secretaries were inside the house, but Mrs. Dallas was not," Moore prompted further disclosures.

"Well, like Miss Remsen, Mrs. Dallas's having a latchkey puts her on an even footing with the people in the house. And I can tell you, anybody with a latchkey could get into that house unheard. I've tried it, and the door latch and lock are so slick and so well oiled that they move with absolute silence. Then the thick, soft rugs in the hall and on the stairs are soundproof, and there's no creaking step anywhere. Of course, all the appointments of that house are perfect, but it's especially true of the precautions taken to eliminate noise."

"Purposely so?"

"I daresay. It may be old Tracy had a special objection to noise and so guarded against it. But that doesn't matter; the fact remains, anybody could go all over that house without making a sound, if careful enough."

"Then, whether the murderer was a member of the household, or a silent intruder from outside, how did he get away from Mr. Tracy's suite of rooms, leaving the outer door of the suite locked behind him?"

March looked Keeley Moore squarely in the face.

"Have you no idea?" he said.

"Have you?" countered Moore.

"Oh, yes, I have. He went out the window."

"Into the lake?"

"Into the lake."

CHAPTER XI

EVIDENCE

The two women, who were eagerly listening, were, of course, more surprised than were Keeley and I, but they were no more chagrined.

I could see Kee's look of blank astonishment, as he heard March's assertion and saw the look of conviction on the detective's face.

"Then," Keeley recovered himself enough to speak coolly, "then, we must look for a master diver, after all."

"Practically, yes," March agreed. "But that doesn't mean a world wonder or a professional champion. It is more to the point that our diver should know the position of the rocks under the windows and the locality of the clear depths."

"Have you any proof of all this?"

"I sure have. Footprints on the window sill, fingerprints on the window frame and a streak of red paint."

"Red paint?"

"Yes, which I take to be the scratch of that Totem thing."

"Why do you take that?"

"Well, to my mind, that Totem means something. You know the old original Totem Poles,—I've been looking up the matter,—had to do with clans or family fealty or something like that."

"You don't seem to be entirely clear about it," Lora said, with a little smile.

"No, ma'am, I'm not. But I'm clear enough to make my point that whoever took that pole took it as a memento or mascot or whatever you like to call it of Sampson Tracy. I mean it made it all a personal matter, not the work of an ordinary burglar."

"No," Kee agreed, "I can't see the earmarks of an ordinary burglar."

"I see what Mr. March is driving at," Maud declared. "He means that the murderer, whoever he was, was one who knew Mr. Tracy, and had known him intimately. One who was either a family connection or a housemate, and who killed his victim for personal reasons rather than for robbery or sordid motives."

"Yes, ma'am," March spoke gratefully, "that's what I mean, partly. And it seems to me like the work of a friend suddenly turned enemy or a calm, self-restrained nature that something roused to the pitch of homicidal mania."

"Ah, psychology——" began Lora, but March interrupted.

"No, ma'am, I don't hold with those modern, hifalutin sciences. Doctor Rogers, now, he knows all about such things, but you didn't hear him referring to anything of the sort. No, I don't mean psychology, but only just the natural working of a brain suddenly roused to ungovernable rage."

"For a reason?"

"For a reason, of course. The reason doubtless being Tracy's refusal of whatever boon the other was asking."

"Then this other may be a relative, a friend or a servant?"

"Yes, always remembering it is a person with an ingenious brain and proficiency in diving and swimming."

"Count 'em up, then," and Moore held up his hand and checked off on his fingers. "Ames, Everett, Griscom——"

"Mrs. Dallas and Miss Remsen," March finished for him.

"Oh, leave out the women," I said, trying to speak lightly, "they can't dive like pearl fishers."

"Miss Remsen can," March asserted, "and it may be that Mrs. Dallas can, though we don't know for certain."

"Well," Lora said, slowly, "give us some more evidence. You can't sit up and reel off names of people. You might as well include Mrs. Merrill and myself."

"No, ma'am, you had no motive. You're not mentioned in the will."

"But surely then, Mrs. Dallas had no motive. She expected to marry Mr. Tracy—why should she want to kill him?"

"Mrs. Dallas is in love with Mr. Everett. She would rather have her legacy and his legacy than to marry Tracy and have the whole works. Mrs. Dallas is not a grasping sort, but she is a woman of deep passions and she is desperately in love with that good-looking young man."

"You seem to know the secrets of their hearts, March," Keeley said. "What about Harper Ames?"

"He's the puzzle." March shook his head. "He's the one I can't make out. He asked you to take on the case, didn't he?"

"He certainly did," Moore stated.

"Well, that's either because he's innocent himself, or because he wants to appear so."

"Can he swim?"

"It's hard to say who can swim and who can't. For those who can, can easily pretend they can't. But that man is as deep as the Sunless Sea, and so far I haven't been able to size him up exactly."

"But look here, March, if you've footprints and fingerprints, what more do you want? Whose are they, anyway?"

"That's another queer thing. They're Miss Remsen's, but she isn't the criminal."

"How do you know?"

"I've talked with her. Now, I'm puzzled about Ames, he's a deep and wily sort. But Miss Remsen is a sweet, innocent young girl, and I'm not so inexperienced that I can't read such. She was scared of me at first, but once I got her calmed down she was straightforward and truthful. I know that, and I'll stand by it."

I could have hugged the man in my joy at his staunch partisanship toward Alma, and I asked more questions.

"Yet you say those were her fingerprints on the window frame?"

He gave me a quick look. "You saw them, then? Yes, they were hers, she was there, you know, on the Tuesday afternoon. Her uncle did say she could have the waistcoats for her fancy work, and he gave her the Totem Pole, too. She had the pole in her hand when she went to open a window, as the room was too warm. She remembered its scratching the white paint, and hoped the mark it made could be washed off."

"And was it the mark of her shoe sole on the window sill?" Keeley asked, and I couldn't judge whether his suave tone was indicative of suspicion or not.

"No, sir, it wasn't!" March sounded triumphant. "Miss Remsen's soles have little round dots in the rubber, these prints showed diamond-shaped dots."

"That lets her out, then," Kee said, drawing a long breath of relief, which made me suddenly realize how strongly he had suspected her.

"It does, but she never was in. That girl couldn't have committed that fearsome crime. It's against all belief! A hardened man of the world, now; or a callous-hearted servant; or even an experienced woman of society; all these sophisticated minds, yes. But that simple-hearted, innocent young girl—no!"

"I agree to that," Lora said, "not only because I want to, but because it's common sense and also psychology. Alma might have shot or stabbed, in a moment of mad rage, but to bring a nail and hammer—it's too absurd."

"Do you think the murderer was abnormal?" Maud said to Keeley.

"To my mind all murderers are abnormal," he replied, thoughtfully. "It surely isn't normal for any one to kill any one else, so, whether temporarily or permanently, to me a murderer is not only abnormal but insane."

"Insane in the sense you mean," March agreed, "that is, on one

93

occasion and on one subject. But that is not what is usually meant by insanity. However, I think we're of the same mind about that."

"Did you see the doughty Merivale when you were at Miss Remsen's house?" Kee asked.

"Yes, and she is a Tartar. She tried to put me off the premises, but Miss Remsen stayed her hand. Also, her better half came to her aid and I had the pair to placate."

"I didn't know the Amazon had a mate."

"Oh, yes. John Merivale, and even bigger and more muscular than 'Merry' herself. Miss Remsen is well protected. They are both her absolute slaves, and except for her intervention would willingly have thrown me in the lake."

"What attitude did you take?"

"Strong arm of the law effect. Said they must answer questions or they'd be haled to court for contempt of same. I scared them good and plenty but I got absolutely no information from them. That is, by word of mouth. But I gleaned a few hints from their unguarded expressions, or their sudden exhibitions of emotion."

"Such as?"

"Nothing very definite. Only their reactions to other people. The two Merivales seem to think in unison. I gathered that they hate Mrs. Dallas, abhor Mr. Ames, tolerate the two secretaries, and are inordinately jealous and envious of all and sundry servants on the Pleasure Dome estate. That, and their worshipful adoration of Miss Remsen herself, is about all I picked up."

"Did you go inside the house or only on the porch?"

"Both. I asked to go inside as it was too damp for my rheumatism outside. But, of course, I saw nothing suspicious. No waistcoats or missing fruit plates. The room I was in was just an ordinary, tastefully furnished living room. A piano, davenport, tables, bookcases, lamps—all such as you'd expect to find in a modern home."

"And the girl lives all alone?"

"Yes. I asked her if she didn't care for a companion or chaperon, and she smiled and said Merry was all those things to her. She seems entirely able to look after herself, and now, she will be mistress of Pleasure Dome, and I think she'll be able to look after that."

"Then you've definitely crossed her off the suspect list?"

"Almost. There's one little point still bothering me, and I shall go again to the Island when both Miss Remsen and her two sentinels are out."

"Can you get such an opportunity?"

"Yes, to-morrow at the time of the funeral. They will, of course, all attend the services and I shall make a small raid on Whistling Reeds. By the way, what a weird, eerie place it is!"

"Isn't it!" Lora cried. "It gives me the shivers just to go past it in the boat. But I must go to call on Alma. Shall we go to-day, Maud?"

"Later, perhaps, dear. I'd like to go, I'm fond of Alma and, like Mr. March, I am sure she never had a hand in this terrible affair."

A maid entered then and announced Mr. Harper Ames.

Keeley looked at March, who nodded, and Ames was shown in.

"Ah, Mr. March, a confab?" he said, after he had greeted the rest of us. "No objections to my joining it, I suppose?"

He took no heed of March's reply, but seated himself comfortably, and accepted the cigar Keeley offered him.

"I have come," he said, speaking slowly and distinctly, "to see if you are investigating the Tracy matter, Mr. Moore. To see what you have accomplished so far and to learn if you hope for success."

His pause and his inquiring glance demanded a reply, and Keeley said, with equal slowness and distinctness:

"Yes, Mr. Ames, I am investigating the Tracy matter. I have accomplished so far only some preliminary work, and I hope for success, of course, or I shouldn't keep on with the case."

"One more question, then. Are you making your investigation at my request, at my expense, and under my direction?"

"No, I think not." Keeley spoke with utmost good nature, but with a decided shake of his head. "You see, it irks me to work for another, if I am interested in a case for myself."

"Why are you so interested in this case?"

Kee stared at him.

"Because it is a case to interest all residents of Deep Lake district. Because murder has been done in our hitherto peaceful community and every right-thinking man must or should be interested. If by my experience and training I am better able than some to look into the facts and indications of the evidence gathered, it is surely my duty to do so, regardless of requests or directions from anybody else."

"Well, then, after all," Ames smiled, "I can't see that it matters much, except that if you're working for me, you get paid for it, if you're on your own, you don't."

I couldn't quite understand this man. Suave, polished, and of gentle voice and correct manners, he now and then broke out with a brusque, blunt speech that seemed to betray a cruder nature beneath his veneer.

Yet he had said nothing really rude, had only stated the bald facts of the matter.

I glanced at March. He too, was covertly studying Ames. I felt sure he was puzzled in the same way I was.

Keeley, however, seemed ready to meet Ames on his own ground.

"Yes," he added, "you've struck it right. Work for you and take your money, or go it alone and get no pay. Well, Mr. Ames, I'm going it alone this trip. But, if I don't take your money, mayn't I ask for something else from you? Won't you give me some advice or some data or some facts you've picked up——"

"Why should I?"

"Because, though I'm not working at your direction, I shall do just as good work, in fact, just the same work as if I were. Therefore, you will get the results the same as if you paid for them. Oughtn't that to make you willing to help in any way you can?"

"But you're assuming I want to save money. You speak as if I should be glad not to have to pay your bill. Not so, Mr. Moore. When I asked you to take me as a client, I was, and am, perfectly willing to shoulder the expenses."

"I see; then, Mr. Ames, the question of price doesn't interest you. Therefore, I ask of you, as you ask of me, to help me with any information you may possess."

"And how do you know I possess any?"

"Because you are afraid. You are not afraid for yourself but for some one else."

It was when Kee was making a statement of this sort that he was at his best. His good-looking face grew positively handsome in its impressive strength and forcefulness.

Only I, and perhaps Lora, knew that it was play acting. Knew that what Keeley Moore said in this histrionic manner was, almost always, merely bluff. He didn't know at all that Ames was shielding some one else, but this was his way of finding out. And nine times out of ten it was successful.

It was this time.

Harper Ames collapsed like a man struck by lightning. He fell back in his seat and turned a sickly white.

I felt sorry for him. It didn't seem quite cricket for Kee to get him like that. I moved toward him, but Moore spoke sharply: "Let him alone, Gray, don't touch him."

That moment, however, had given Ames time to pull himself together.

Also, his insolent manner returned to him.

"I get you, Moore," he said, with an unpleasant laugh. "We are enemies, then? So be it. You have turned me down, now I turn you down, and the thing I came to tell you, you will never know. The investigation you propose to make will be futile; the success you so confidently hope for you will never achieve."

The man was very angry. Indeed, his rage was a revelation to me. I had not supposed him capable of such fierce passions. It flashed across my mind that a man like that could murder on a sudden provocation.

But now March took a hand.

"Mr. Ames," the police detective said, in a quiet way, "you have said too much not to say more. Since you admitted you came here to tell something, you are obliged to tell it."

"And if I refuse?"

"You will be called upon to tell it to the chief of police."

"And if I still refuse?"

"I think you know for yourself the consequences of such a procedure."

Ames sat silent a few moments and then he said:

"Oh, I don't want any unpleasantness. My speech was partly bluff, but what there is to it, I am quite willing to tell you. It is only that after I went to my room that night, after leaving Mr. Tracy, I heard sounds, of which I have not told."

"Important sounds?"

"That's as may be. How do I know? I heard, or I thought I heard, a step on the stair."

"Are you sure, Mr. Ames?" asked March. "For I cannot manage to make a step that is audible on those softly carpeted stairs at Pleasure Dome."

Ames looked at him in surprise.

"Is that so? Well, it may have been a step in the hall——"

"Nor along the thick carpet of the hall——" went on March, as if he had not been interrupted.

"You're trying to say I lie," Ames cried out. "But it is true. I will not say, then, what the sound was, but I did hear a slight sound outside my door a little before two o'clock——"

"Did it waken you?" March spoke eagerly.

"N-no, I was awake—I think. But I heard it distinctly, though very faintly. It was like——"

"Yes, what was it like? You said, like a step."

"No, not like a step—like a gliding, shuffling movement and a—a——"

"Go on."

"Like a stick or something dragged across my door."

"Dragged?"

"Oh, I mean, drawn across my door,—here, like this."

Ames, with a petulant gesture, picked up an ivory paper cutter from the table and drew it leisurely across a cupboard door, making a slight rattling sound.

"Yes," he said, nodding his head satisfiedly, "just like that."

"As if some one were passing your door, and idly drew across it something he had in his hand?"

"Yes, just that."

"Why haven't you told this before?"

"I attached no importance to it. In fact, I had forgotten it."

"And what brought it again to your mind?"

"Nothing especial. I was going over the events of that night, to think if there was anything else I could tell Mr. Moore. I didn't know he was going to throw me!"

Keeley laughed outright. Ames spoke so like an aggrieved child.

"I haven't thrown you, Mr. Ames," he declared. "I'm sure you and I are going to work together. I'm awfully interested in the chap who drummed along your door. I believe it was the murderer himself."

"You do!" Ames turned a friendly look on Kee. "Then you can run him down?"

"I hope so. Now, tell us, who is it you're shielding?"

"Nobody. Honest. But this sound in the hall was worrying my conscience."

"I see. I see." And I knew that Keeley Moore had crossed Harper Ames definitely off his list of suspects.

Doubtless he was right. Kee was seldom wrong.

But I was worried. I was getting to the pitch where I was always worried—about Alma. Oh, if only I hadn't seen her go to Pleasure Dome that night! Or if I could find an innocent reason for her going. Or if she hadn't denied on the witness stand that she did go.

Anyhow, it was plain to be seen that not only Keeley Moore but Detective March had exonerated Ames in their minds, and that because of Ames's own frank relation of a hitherto suppressed bit of evidence.

"All a fake," I said, angrily, to myself. "He's pulling wool over their eyes!" But I knew better. Even to my untrained intelligence, Ames's story had rung true. He had heard the sound in the hall, and no one who heard his tale could doubt it.

Then Ames rose to go, and somehow, I found myself by Maud's side walking down to the gate with our caller.

"Do come over again, Mr. Ames," Maud said, hospitably, as she bade him good-bye.

And then Ames went off and March came along on his way out.

Maud stopped him to speak a moment, and I half turned aside.

Had I known what the result of her words would be, I think I should have choked her to silence ere I let her utter them!

But I only heard her say, casually: "Then you will not be at the funeral, Mr. March?"

"No, Mrs. Merrill. I think it too good a chance to lose to do two or three errands I have in mind."

"One of them being to search Miss Remsen's home?"

"That's almost too strong a phrase. But I mean to take a run over there and see what I can get from the other servants when the two Merivales are away."

"Then, do this, Mr. March, will you? Glance over the bookcase and see if you notice a book of short stories—detective stories, you know. The title is Mystery Tales of All Nations, Volume VIII."

"Is it your book?"

"Oh, no, I don't know that it's there at all. Just see, that's all."

"Yes, ma'am, I will," and March went away.

Angrily, I turned on Maud Merrill.

"Have you got it in for Alma?" I exclaimed.

"Mercy, no! Don't look at me like that, Gray Norris! I'm only trying to get any information I can. And I still think that story is at the bottom of this murder!"

"Trust a woman to get a fool idea into her head and stick to it like a puppy to a root!" I cried, scowling at her.

But she only laughed at me, and changed the subject.

CHAPTER XII

MY SECRET

We went back into the house and Maud, with a smile at me, said:

"Keeley, I asked our super-sleuth, March, to scout around for a stray copy of that book that has in it the story of The Nail, and Graysie, here, is mad at me."

"Nonsense!" I cried, "I'm not. But I daresay there were some thousands of copies of the book printed, and if, when and as you find one, you can't at once assume that you have hit upon the murderer of Sampson Tracy."

"That story is Maud's angle of the case," Kee said. "Her own exclusive property and she must be allowed to exploit it as she likes. I'm free to confess I haven't much faith in it as a pointer, but I will say if the book is found on the bedside table of any one who benefits by Sampson Tracy's death, it will be a lead that must be followed up."

"Oh, all right," I said, grumpily. "I can see you all suspect Alma Remsen more or less, but why don't you come out and say so?"

"Gray," Keeley spoke a little sternly, "you've fallen in love with Miss Remsen, and while that's your own affair, you mustn't assume that it at once absolves her from all suspicion in this matter. Now, wait a minute before you explode. I don't say the girl is suspected of crime, but there is a possibility that she knows something she hasn't told, just as Ames knew about that step in the hall, and just as you know something that wild horses couldn't drag out of you."

"What do you mean?" I spluttered, angry and ashamed at the same time.

"You know what I mean. You have some bit of knowledge or information that you have been on the point of telling me half a dozen times, and then have concluded not to do so. I'm not asking you what it is, I'm not saying it is your duty to tell. That's your business. But I do say you have no right to cavil at anything I may do in the interests of justice, and no reason to get upset if my investigations tend toward Alma Remsen's connection with the case."

I was in love, I was upset, but after all, my sense of fairness was still with me.

"You're right, Kee," I said. "And I will not again let my admiration for Miss Remsen come into the question. Except where it concerns her, I am ready to help, if I can, with your work, and I am sure you can give me chores to do, away from that line of inquiry. Let me interview others, there must be others, and you will find that I am not the fool you think me."

"There, there, bless the boy," Maud patted my arm, and though I might have resented her manner in another there was something about her kindly sympathy that made me welcome her friendly interest.

"Of course I think you a fool, Gray," Moore assured me. "I've always thought so. But, aren't we all?"

"Of course we are," chimed in Lora. "I wouldn't give a fig for anyone who wasn't a fool in some ways. Now, don't think, Gray, your shy avowal is news to us, for we knew you had fallen for the lovely Alma almost before you knew it yourself. And we all approve, and look forward to a happy ending. But for the moment, we are engrossed in another matter. And though Keeley says he is not going to urge you to tell us the secret you are withholding, I am, and I hope you will feel that it is better to let us know it."

I thought a minute and then I said:

"Lora, you're a dear, and I can scarce refuse you anything at all. But this thing I know, which may mean something or nothing, is so trivial, so insignificant that I do not feel guilty in keeping it quiet, at least for a little time longer. Moreover, its weight, if it has any, would be against Alma's interests, so please think I am justified in keeping still."

"You are, Gray," Keeley said, heartily. "The more so, that I do not ask for evidence against the girl. If she is implicated at all, we have enough evidence, what we want is admission on her part. So, keep your bit of information and should it become really necessary I'll demand it."

He nodded his head so understandingly that I saw we were reëstablished on the old footing, and I rejoice that I had not told my secret.

For, whatever they said, I felt sure that a statement that I had seen Alma go to Pleasure Dome that fatal night at about one-thirty and had probably heard her return about two-thirty, would be something like a match to a trail of gunpowder.

"Now," Keeley went on, "I must do some real Sherlocking. First, as to Harper Ames. I'm inclined to scratch his name from my list of suspects because of his frankly expressed desire that I should take the case for him. Either he has the knowledge of his own absolute innocence, or else he is the very most clever devil I have ever chanced to run across."

"He's innocent all right," Lora said. "He couldn't act out all that.

101

He really wants you to take the case, Kee, and that proves his innocence."

"But does it?" Moore argued. "May it not be that he is the guilty man and he is bold enough to think that by taking such a course he can steer suspicion away from himself?"

"Seems to me," I put in, "that for a real Sherlock you are doing a lot of theorizing and surmising. Why not get down to shreds of wool, missing cuff-links and dropped handkerchiefs?"

"Keeley isn't a fictional detective," Lora exclaimed. "He doesn't work on conventional lines——"

"There are two kinds of fictional detectives, my dear girl," Keeley told her. "The detective of fiction, and the story-book sleuth who declares that he is not the detective of fiction. The original detective of fiction was the hound-on-the-scent sort. The man who could put two and two together. The wizard who could tell the height, weight, and colouring of the unknown criminal from a flick of cigar ash. Then, as this superman palled a bit on the reader, came then his successor, the man who scorned all these tricks of the trade and announced himself as not the detective of fiction."

"And which sort are you?" asked Lora, brightly, with a hint of veiled chaffing.

"I'm a mixture of both," Kee stated calmly. "But I do think one should consider the bent and inclination of a suspect as well as the material clues he leaves about."

"For instance?" I asked.

"All that stuff left on the bed. Your old Sherlock type would say: 'These flowers were placed here by an ex-gardener, with red hair and a missing little finger.' But to my mind, the deduction would be that the flowers were put there by a man the farthest possible remove from an ex-gardener, rather, a man of keen, sharp wits and decided ingenuity."

"Merely as a blind, or, rather as a misleading clue?" I suggested.

"Yes. Now, the superfluity of those things on the bed, I mean the multiplicity of them, betokens a nature inclined to overdo. Like a man who, getting on a steam-boat, ties himself on."

"Or," put in Lora, "if a man compel thee to go a mile, go with him twain."

"Yes, something of that sort. Yet it may be that he started on his mad career of bed decorating and went on and on, sort of absent-mindedly."

"Got started and couldn't stop."

"Exactly. Say he placed the flowers first, then, seeing the orange and crackers, added those, then, noticing the crucifix, used that;

102

then the handkerchief, and finally draped the scarf round them all, just because it was handy by."

"And the watch in the pitcher?"

"Oh, that dratted thing! That throws the whole matter into another category. That watch is my hope and my stumbling block, both."

"You've been mysterious before, Kee, about that watch. Now out with it. What's the separate mystery of the watch in the pitcher?"

"Quid pro quo," said Kee, smiling at me. "You tell me what you're concealing up your sleeve and I'll divulge the dark hint suggested to me by the watch."

I hesitated, but my disinclination to tell of the canoe incident was too strong. I couldn't bring myself to let loose a torrent of suspicion that might engulf Alma.

"Can't do it," I said, honestly. "I would, if I thought it my duty as a citizen or as your friend, Kee. But, as I see it, it's better left untold."

"You remind me," Kee said, smiling, "of Jurgen, who said, 'I do my duty as I see it. But there is a tendency in my family toward defective vision.' That isn't quoted verbatim, but nearly so. All right, old son, keep your guilty secret and I'll keep mine."

"Do. What's next on your sleuthing program?"

"I'm going to interview Mrs. Dallas."

"How will she like that?"

"I daresay she won't be any too well pleased. But, unless she refuses to see us, we can't help learning something. Will you go with me?"

"Of course," I returned, glad he wanted me. I truly desired to help, so long as the work didn't touch on the girl I cared for.

The talk with them about her had, in a way, crystallized my feelings, and I knew now I loved her, a fact of which I had before been only vaguely aware.

Also, I was prepared to fight for her. And if the fight could be helped on by incriminating some one else, so much the better.

We started for Mrs. Dallas's home, which was only a short walk along the lake shore.

Keeley was quiet as usual, and gave me fully to understand that he bore no ill will over my refusal to confide in him more fully.

"You see, Gray," he said, talking things over with me in the old, friendly fashion, "there's no use blinking the accepted fact that those who benefit most by the death of a rich man are the ones to be suspected. I know how you feel about Alma, but as you care for her, you, of course, deem her innocent. Therefore you can't feel that she is in any danger from an investigation by detectives. If I were you I should welcome all possible questioning of her, feeling sure that she would have satisfactory explanation for anything that might seem suspicious."

"That's all very well, Kee, if the detectives were not such dunderheaded idiots. You know I don't mean you, but that March Hare and that Hart that panted at the inquest, have it in for the girl, and they are ready to turn anything she may say against her."

"Oh, not so bad as that. But it complicates things, your having gone dotty over her."

"Sorry for the complications, but not sorry for the rest of it. I say, old man, do you suppose she'd look at me?"

"She might do worse," said Kee, as he eyed me appraisingly.

Although he spoke lightly I welcomed his words as a good omen and turned in at the Dallas place, determined to do all I could to help him.

It was a pleasant cottage, unpretentious and homelike, and we were admitted by a trim-looking maid, and conducted to a small reception room.

"Come over here," said a voice, a moment later, and we saw Katherine Dallas smiling at us from the door of the big living room opposite.

She was charming, both in appearance and manner, and greeted us with courtesy if not warmth.

But she clearly showed she considered it an interview rather than a social call and waited for Kee to state his errand.

"Mr. Ames has asked me to look into the matter of Mr. Tracy's death," Moore began, shamelessly hiding behind Ames's skirts. "And though I regret the necessity, I feel I must ask you a few questions which I hope you will be gracious enough to answer."

"Yes," she returned, not at all helpfully, though in no way forbidding.

I saw by the play of Keeley's features that he had sized her up and had concluded to carry on the interview in strictly business fashion.

"You were Mr. Tracy's fiancée at the time of his death?" he asked.

"Yes, Mr. Moore, I was."

"Then, as such, as the one holding the nearest relationship to him, if we except his niece, Miss Remsen, am I correct in assuming you desire the discovery of the criminal who is responsible for his death?"

"No, Mr. Moore, you are not correct in that assumption. I loved Mr. Tracy, I hoped to marry him, but now that he is dead, I should greatly prefer that the matter be considered a closed book. I am not of a vindictive nature and to me the horrors of an investigation and all the harrowing details of such a procedure would be only less distressing than the tragedy itself. So far as I am concerned, I should infinitely prefer that the name of the wretch who cruelly killed Sampson Tracy should be buried in oblivion to having it sought for and blazoned to the public gaze."

"This is not the usual view to take of such a situation, Mrs. Dallas." Kee's tone conveyed distinct reproach.

"The usual view has never meant anything to me, nor does it in this instance."

She was not exactly flippant, but there was a note in her voice that proved, to my mind at least, that she resented any discussion of her mental attitude, and indeed, resented the whole interview and our presence.

Clearly, no help could be expected from her, yet I was moved to put a few straightforward questions.

"Are you remaining here, Mrs. Dallas, for the rest of the summer?"

She favoured me with a glance that was strongly disapproving of such an intrusive remark, and answered, icily:

"That I have not yet decided."

"You know the terms of the will?" Kee shot at her, suddenly, having decided, as he afterward told me, that she was unworthy of delicate consideration.

"Yes," she said, with a face void of expression.

"Then, as one of the principal beneficiaries, you know that you cannot expect to escape definite questioning by the detectives."

"I do not expect to escape it, nor do I fear it. Why are you telling me this, Mr. Moore?"

"I thought you understood that as Mr. Ames's adviser, I must make certain inquiries in the course of pursuing my duties."

She thawed a little, and said, half apologetically, "I suppose so. Is there anything else I can tell you?"

"Yes, Mrs. Dallas. Since Mr. Tracy is dead, have you any intention of marrying any one else?"

"I think, Mr. Moore, you are carrying your zeal for Mr. Ames's work too far. I must beg to be excused from further conversation."

She rose and stood, like a tragedy queen, not angry, but with a scornful look on her handsome face and an expression in her eyes eloquent of dismissal. She did not point to the door, but such a gesture was not necessary with that look in her eyes.

Courteously and with no effect of chagrin, Kee bowed his adieu and I followed suit.

"Whew!" I remarked, after we had regained the outer road, "some goddess!"

"Amazon! Boadicea! Xantippe! Medea!—yes, and Lucrezia Borgia!" he exclaimed, his voice making up in emphasis what it lacked in sound. "This case begins to look interesting, Gray. What price Everett and the Dallas in cahoots as murderers?"

"Are you serious?" I asked, thinking he was merely smarting under the lady's stinging rebuke.

"No, I don't think so. There are more likely suspects. But we learned a lot there. I honestly hated to bang her between the eyes as I did, but she was just about to order us out anyway, and I had to find out her state of mind regarding Everett."

"And did you?"

"Of course I did. Her sudden flush of colour and the ghastly fear that came into her eyes for an instant told me the truth. Gray, she not only loves Charles Everett, but she is not at all certain that he is not the murderer."

"That lets her out, then."

"Oh, of course.... She never committed murder. And, she was at home in bed when the deed was done. She was at our party that night, you know."

"Yes, I know, but she went home early."

"Oh, well, there's not the slightest suspicion attached to her. When I said in cahoots, I didn't really mean it, or, if I did, I look on her as merely a sleeping partner. But I think she is entirely innocent of crime, or even accessory work, and I think, too, that she fears for Everett. Maybe not that he did the deed, but that he may be suspected of it. I don't like the woman, I never did, but I think she's innocent of any real wrong. I think she was engaged to Tracy for purely mercenary reasons, then Everett came along, and she fell for him, and she is now glad that old Samp is out of the way, but she didn't bring it about."

"Probably you're right, Kee, but I don't hanker after any more calls on suspects if they're going to be as strenuous as that."

"Oh, that's nothing—all in the day's work. All right, then, if you're off the case for to-day. I'm going over to Whistling Reeds, but you can toddle home, if you like."

"You're going there? To Alma's? Indeed I will go with you. What are you going for?"

"On a quest for knowledge and information." He spoke gravely.

"Are you going to torment her, Kee?" I asked.

"Not intentionally. But I must ask some questions and she must answer. Now, go or stay away, as you choose."

"I'll go," I said, and we walked a while in silence.

Reaching our own boathouse, Kee chose his favourite round-bottomed boat and we started for the Island.

I rowed, for I felt the need of some physical exertion to calm my racing nerves, stirred by the thought of the ordeal ahead of us.

Keeley had not suspected Mrs. Dallas—he said so—but I had a feeling he did suspect Alma, and I wondered what his attitude would be.

"Don't be harsh with her," I said, at last, apparently apropos of nothing.

"I'm not utterly a brute," he returned, and I bent to my oars.

It was a gray day. The clouds hid the sun entirely and they were dull heavy clouds, not fleecy white ones such as I loved. The lake was leaden, and the ripples waved slowly but did not break into whitecaps.

There were no other boats in sight and no crowds of merry people on the few docks we passed.

Reaching the Remsen boathouse, it seemed to me the Island looked more than ever like an abode of the dead. The trees were motionless in the calm air and the dark glades and copses seemed sepulchral in their sentinel-like rigidity.

We landed and went up the steps toward the house.

A man advanced to meet us.

"What's wanted?" he said, not quite gruffly, but with an apparent intention of being answered.

"We want to see Miss Remsen," Kee replied and his manner was suavity itself. "I am Keeley Moore, from Variable Winds, down the lake. This is my friend, Mr. Norris. Take us to the house, Mr. Merivale, and announce us to Miss Remsen."

"Announce you, is it? When I'm tellin' you she isn't home!"

He hadn't told us that before, but he seemed to think he had, and he stood directly in our path, so that we could advance no step.

"Where is she, please?"

"She and Merry—that's my wife, sir—have gone down to the village."

"And nobody's home?"

"Nobody but me and one or two kitchen servants."

"Well, let us sit on the porch a few moments. Mr. Norris is all tuckered out with his row over here, and I've got to row back. So, maybe you'll give us a drink of water; if Mrs. Merivale was at home, I'd ask for tea."

The strange-looking man seemed to relent a little.

He was an enormous, strapping fellow, not fierce-looking but of powerful build and a strong, forceful countenance. He gazed at us out of deep-set eyes overhung with shaggy eyebrows of stiff gray hair.

"Come along, then," he said. "You can sit on the porch, and I'll make you a cup of tea. I can make better tea than Merry."

But as he turned to leave us, he said, with a slight smile:

"If so be you gentlemen could put up with a drop of Scotch and soda, it'd save me boilin' the kettle."

We agreed to put up with the substitute, and he went off.

We said little during the old man's absence. I felt relieved that Kee did not insist on going into the house, and I sat looking about at the beautiful though gloomy landscape.

Yet, viewed from the porch, it was not so bad. The flower beds gave enough colour, and the near-by trees were mostly white birch, with their graceful shapes and pale, lovely trunks.

Yet between us and the lake was a solid wall of dark, dense woodland that shut off all view of the outer world and shut in the Island and its buildings and people.

"I can't see why Alma likes this place," I said, in a low voice. "She doesn't seem at all morbid or despondent herself."

"Do you know her?" Keeley asked me, and I suddenly realized that I didn't know her at all! But, I promised myself, that was a defect that time should remedy and that, I hoped, soon.

From where I sat, I could see into the house through a window. I looked into the same room we had been in the other day I had called here, the day when Merry had told us if we were men to let the poor girl alone.

As I looked, not curiously, only idly, I saw the old man, Merivale, come into the room and adjust a record and then turn on a victrola.

The strains of Raff's Cavatina floated out to us, and Kee gave a little smile of enjoyment.

A moment later, Merivale appeared with glasses on a tray, and I said, pleasantly, "Your music sounds fine, out here on the lake."

He looked up suddenly, saw the open window and frowned.

"That Katy!" he exclaimed. "She's forever turnin' on that machine! Do you mind it, sir?" He looked anxiously at Kee.

"No," was the reply, but I marvelled as to why this cheerful old liar should put the blame on poor, innocent Katy, for a deed that I had seen him do himself.

CHAPTER XIII

AS TO TUESDAY AFTERNOON

And then Alma came home.

I watched her as she paddled her canoe, with long, clear-cut strokes, and I remembered what Billy Dean had said about her paddling being unmistakable.

Perhaps this was an exaggeration, but surely her method was that of an expert. She brought the pretty, graceful craft to a landing and sprang out, followed more leisurely by the gaunt figure of the ever-watchful Merry.

She wore an exceedingly becoming sports costume of white with borderings of black, and a little white felt hat with a black cockade.

I watched her as she came nearer and I realized anew that this was the one girl in the world for me. And I knew, too, that she needed a friend, needed some one to lean on, in the ordeal that was ahead of her. For whatever the outcome of the inquest, she faced new responsibilities and burdens in the adjustment of her uncle's estate.

I suppose a more conscientious nature would have hesitated to aspire to a girl set apart by a sudden acquisition of great wealth, but I was too deeply in love to think of that. I had a competent income myself, and I should have been glad to marry Alma Remsen had she been penniless, but all those considerations were as nothing to the all-absorbing thought of how I loved her.

She was so appealing as she raised her eyes to mine, when she greeted me, and her sweet face was so wistful, that it was all I could do to keep from grabbing her up in my arms and carrying her off.

As it was, I took her hand and made conventional inquiries, the while devouring her with my eyes.

I think she sensed my restraint, for her handclasp was friendly, even trustful, and we sat down together on a porch settee.

"You're a frequent caller, Mr. Moore," she said, almost gaily. "I'm sorry I was so unsatisfactory on the occasion of your other visit; I'll try to do better this time."

I looked at her in some apprehension. I felt sure her light manner was assumed, to cover the depths of worry and anxiety that, it seemed to me, showed themselves in her dark eyes.

"I don't want to bother you too much, Miss Remsen," Keeley said, "but you can be a real help, if you choose."

"Of course I choose. Ask me anything you like—I'll answer."

She gave a little smile and tossed her head with a pretty gesture.

Both the Merivales had disappeared. I had an uncanny feeling that they were watching from behind some window curtain, but I had no real reason for this. The victrola had ceased its music—doubtless Katy had turned it off.

"It's about that last call you made on your uncle," Keeley proceeded, and I could see he was watching her closely, though he seemed not to do so. "It was the last time you saw him alive, was it not? That Tuesday afternoon?"

"Yes," said Alma, in a quiet, steady voice. "Yes, that was the last time."

"What did you go there for?"

"On no especial errand; only to see him. I always go over two or three times a week, or thereabouts."

"And, according to Mr. March, you raised a window in your uncle's sitting room, thereby leaving your fingerprints on the white enamel paint?"

"So Mr. March told me. I know little of fingerprints—I mean as evidence—but I well know how they mar white paint. I am a tidy housekeeper, and I am continually at war with fingerprints on white paint."

I glanced around the porch and looked through the window into the living room. Everything was immaculate and I could well believe that the girl made a fetish of tidiness.

"Yes. Then it scarcely seems like you to have your hands in such condition that they would leave marks on the window frame."

"No, it doesn't seem like me." Alma lifted her lovely little hands one after the other and scrutinized them with apparent interest. "No, I rarely have dirty hands. Even as a child, Merry says I was always tidy. But, Mr. Moore, I'm told that fingerprints cannot be mistaken, and so the fact remains, doesn't it, that on that particular occasion my hands did need washing?"

There was a certain something in Alma's voice that drew my attention. She seemed to be speaking casually, seemed really indifferent as to the subject, yet her tone was alert and her whole manner tense. It was almost as if she was studying the effect of her words on Moore far more intently than he was studying her. Yet, this was absurd. Why should she fear him? She had already admitted and explained the fingerprints to March, who had expressed himself satisfied.

"You went to the window, then, to raise it in order to let more air into the room?"

"Yes."

"Didn't it rain in?"

"What?" the suddenness of her exclamation made me jump.

"Yes," Keeley went on, "there was a hard shower Tuesday afternoon, and it came from the east. It should have rained right in that window."

"Then it was before or after the shower," Alma said, but she faltered a little. "For it certainly did not rain in."

"At what time were you there?"

"I don't remember exactly. After lunch and before tea time."

"You usually have afternoon tea, Miss Remsen?"

"Yes. Merry, my nurse, is English and she enjoys it, so we've made it a habit. I've grown to like it."

"Then, you were doubtless at your uncle's on Tuesday, sometime, say, between two o'clock and five."

"Yes, that must be right."

"You went and returned in your canoe?"

"Yes."

"And it was not raining when you went, or when you came home, or when you opened that window?"

"No."

"But, Miss Remsen, it is an established fact that it rained all that afternoon, from one till six o'clock. This is verified by the weather statistics."

Only for a moment did Alma look blank. Then she said, quickly:

"Oh, really? Then I must be mistaken in the day. I must have been there Monday afternoon. The days fly by so swiftly in summer, I can hardly keep track of them."

"Perhaps," said Kee, looking a bit baffled. "But another strange thing—Griscom says those fingerprints were not on the white paint Wednesday evening when he put the suite in order for the night. He says he would surely have seen them if they had been."

She gave a little light laugh. "Poor old Griscom. His eyes are not what they used to be, I daresay. Now, Mr. Moore, just what is it you want me to say? Am I proving an alibi? Or are you trying to trick me into a confession that I killed my uncle? Because, I didn't, and though I may be hazy about the exact time of my last visit to him, I did go over there——"

"And he did give you the satin waistcoats?"

"Yes," but now her eyelids quivered, "he did give me the satin waistcoats."

"And you did open that window?"

"Yes," she spoke slowly.

"And you had in your hand the Totem Pole and it chanced to make a red mark on the side of the window frame?"

"Yes—yes, I did."

"Well, none of these things is incriminating in any way. Now, go on, please, why did you step up on the window sill?"

"I didn't!" A look of horror came into her eyes.

"But there is the mark of a sole there, a rubber sole. No, not those shoes you have on now," he glanced at her crossed feet, "but shoes whose rubber soles show a design of little diamond-shaped dots."

Alma took an appreciable moment to collect herself and then said calmly, "I don't own any such shoes as you describe, Mr. Moore."

"Are you willing I should glance through your wardrobe?"

I could have slain Keeley with decided relish, but Alma seemed to take no offence. She paused an instant, as if considering, then said:

"Certainly. Shall I take you to my dressing room?"

"No, please. Will you remain here with Mr. Norris and let a maid show me the way? I'm sorry, but believe me, Miss Remsen, frankness is your best card. Please play it."

As this was accompanied by Kee's kindest smile and most winning manner, I was not greatly surprised to see an answering smile on Alma's face.

"Merry," she called out, but in a tone so little above her speaking voice I was surprised to see the woman appear at once. Yet I might have known she was within listening distance.

"Merry, dear," Alma said, "Mr. Moore has occasion to look over my shoe cabinet. Are all my shoes in it?"

"Yes, Miss Alma, except the ones you are wearing."

"Then take Mr. Moore upstairs and give him all the assistance he requires."

It was easy enough to see that Merry was not rejoiced over her errand, but she nodded assent and led the way into the house.

No sooner had they disappeared than I seized my opportunity. It might be I should never again get such a good chance.

"Alma," I said, breathlessly, "I love you—oh, my darling, how I love you! Now, wait a minute, don't look at me as if I had lost my mind, and don't, for Heaven's sake, call help! I have loved you from the first moment I saw you, and my love grows stronger every moment that passes. You may not love me—yet—but you will some day. I'll see to that. So, for the present, just accept the situation as it is, and let me help you. I can't help thinking you do not realize the danger you are in. The detective March is for you, but Keeley Moore is out for investigation, and when he gets started nothing ever stops

112

him. If you have anything to hide, anything to conceal, give it to me. I will help you in any way and every way I can."

Had I been less excited, I should have enjoyed the passing emotions that played successively across her face. Amazement, happiness, wonder, fear, terror and after all, a beautiful trust, that told me more than all the rest.

"Gray," she said, "I shall love you some day, I promise you that, now, but first, you must, you will help me! I am in danger, I can't explain all to you now, I'm not sure I ever can, but in one matter you must help me. There is something I want destroyed, something that must be destroyed. Will you attend to that?"

"Of course I will. Give it to me quickly. Is it small enough to throw into the lake?"

"Small enough, yes. But it won't sink. Weight it, and throw it in the lake when nobody can possibly see you, or else burn it—but you couldn't do that?"

"Not very well, as I am visiting friends. But give it to me, and I'll see to it that it is destroyed at once."

"I hoped to do it myself, but I think—I fear I am being watched. When I went to the village with Merry, a man in a canoe seemed to follow and he watched me, yet tried to look as if he were not watching me. Oh, I know."

"Did you object to Moore's questioning?"

"Oh, no." She looked weary and a little sad. "I suppose I must go through with a lot of that."

"Do you mind his looking at your wardrobe?"

"No," she smiled at this. "What does he expect to find? I haven't any other rubber-soled shoes. I've ordered a new tan pair, but they haven't come home yet."

She scrutinized her little white canvas shoe, and as she held it up, I noticed the pattern of round dots on the rubber sole.

"Give me what you want thrown away," I whispered. "I think I hear Moore's step. And, Alma, I must see you, unhurried and alone. Can't you meet me some evening late—some night soon—out on the lake?"

What possessed me to say that, I don't know, but it seemed to strike her like a blow.

"Oh, no," she said, and fairly shuddered. "Don't suggest such a thing! I never go on the lake after sundown."

This, when I had seen her canoeing after midnight!

Well, all that must some time be explained, and I rushed on:

"Then, let's not keep it secret, but announce our engagement at once, and I can look after you."

"Mercy, no! What an idea. But here, here is the thing I want

113

destroyed. Not only thrown away, it must be instantly and secretly destroyed."

"As you destroyed the shoes," I said, involuntarily.

"Yes," she returned, gravely, almost solemnly, "as I destroyed the shoes."

From a handbag she had brought with her and had laid on the settee she drew a small book, a worn, paper-covered volume, which she hurriedly thrust into my hand, her eyes turned to the house, where we could now hear the nurse and Keeley coming downstairs.

I stuffed the book into my overcoat, glad that I had with me the light topcoat I usually carried against the chill winds of Deep Lake.

Then, quickly folding the coat inside out, I threw it over a chair back just as Keeley reappeared.

"Thank you very much, Miss Remsen," he said, cheerily. "Your willingness to put the whole house at my disposal makes me more sure you have nothing to conceal than any words you could say."

"But I didn't put the whole house at your disposal!" she exclaimed with mock dismay.

"But your good nurse did. She took me on a whirlwind voyage of discovery, and I discovered absolutely nothing——"

"Not even the shoes?" Alma looked positively roguish now, and very alluring.

"Not even the shoes," Kee repeated. "Nor the Totem Pole. What became of that?"

All Alma's gayety fell away from her. She showed again that fear that so often darkened her eyes and clouded her brow.

But she shrugged her shoulders lightly, and said, "Oh, it's around somewhere—it must be."

"Never mind," Kee said, kindly, "it doesn't really matter."

"You saw the waistcoats?"

"Yes, they were lying on the bed in the guest room. If you're like my wife, you use the guest-room bed for a general temporary repository."

"Every woman does," Alma smiled, but it was a pitiful little smile. More than ever I longed to capture her bodily and carry her off from this situation that was so rapidly growing worse. I knew Kee so well that I felt sure he had discovered far more than he disclosed, and my heart throbbed at thought of his possible future disclosures.

We came away then, after a little more good-natured, chaffing banter between Alma and Keeley.

Merry stood in the background. Her quick eyes darted from one to another of us, but her expression was one of satisfaction and content, and I realized that if Kee had found anything, Merry didn't suspect it.

He bade Alma good-bye in cordial, pleasant fashion, and I did the same. I could show my feelings in no way save to press her hand and gaze deeply into her eyes, and having accomplished this histrionic gesture, I turned to find Kee looking at me with full comprehension of the situation.

I didn't mind that, for he already knew I was in love with her, so, aside from a slight sheepish feeling, I was unembarrassed as I strode along by his side down to the dock. Old Merivale was ahead of us, to push us off, so Kee said nothing, but he nudged my elbow and pointed significantly to some footprints in the dust of the path. We were walking between some flower beds in preference to the gravel walk, and the prints were, in many instances, clear and distinct.

They had been made by a small shoe, obviously a woman's shoe, whose rubber sole showed little diamond-shaped dots.

There could be no doubt about it. The prints were too plain to be mistaken by either of us.

Keeley said no word, but he made sure I saw and understood their importance.

I was sick at heart at the way things were going, but with an undercurrent of gladness that Alma had not repulsed my love. True, she had not definitely accepted it, either, but I was willing to bide my time.

Old Merivale deftly assisted us into our craft and gave us a shove off. I rowed, at Keeley's request.

"Isn't it your turn, lazybones?" I asked him.

"No, you row," he returned, in a preoccupied tone, and willingly enough I plied the oars.

After we had rounded a bend of the shore, and were out of sight of the Remsen house, he said, very seriously:

"So you proposed to compound a felony, Gray?"

All at once, I remembered the book Alma had given me to destroy. I had forgotten it for the few moments we were taking leave, but I didn't blame myself for that, as I considered it hidden in my overcoat pocket, and my overcoat, folded inside out completely protected it. Had Keeley found it?

"What do you mean?"

"That's the proper response. Well, I mean, when a lady gives you a book to destroy, why don't you destroy it?"

He sat in the stern, facing me and steering. As I looked at him, ready to give vent to my wrath, he said, with a friendly smile:

"Hold on, Gray. Don't fly off the handle. Do you know what the book is?"

"No, I don't, but I can tell you——"

"If you can't tell me the name of the book, nothing you can tell me is of any consequence. Can't you guess the title?"

His grave tone and serious face gave me a hint. I stared at him, unbelieving.

"You don't mean——" I stammered.

"Of course I do. It is Detective Stories of All Nations, Volume VIII." He held it up, and then my rage boiled over.

"You—you took that from my pocket!"

"Of course I did. And I shall keep an eye on you after this. Gray, try to recognize what you are doing. Try to recognize what I am doing. Or to put it plainer, remember that I am doing only my duty, and you—are obstructing my honest efforts."

His straightforward glance and his friendly smile won the day, and I mumbled miserably, "What can I do, Kee? I love her so."

"I know, I know, and it complicates matters terribly."

"Shall I go away, back to New York?"

"That would be the best plan, but I know you won't do it."

"No," I said, "I won't do it."

"Then, if you stay here, I mean, if you stay with us, you've got to play fair."

"Fair by you or fair by Alma?"

"Both. Don't think, boy, that I don't understand. But I can't have my work blocked by your interference. Heretofore, you've been a help on my cases——"

"But this is different!" I cried.

"Yes, this is different. So, since you won't go back to New York, and I don't want you to stay at Deep Lake under any other roof but ours, what's the answer?"

Putting it up to me like this, I couldn't combat him or even rebuff him. He was playing fair, all his cards on the table. I must in all honour and justice do likewise. "It would be horrid," I said, at last, "to stay here at the Inn, or anything like that. And I can't—Oh, Kee, I can't go back to New York. But I most certainly propose to play the game. Now, I can only say that if I learn anything further about Alma that I think you want to know, I will tell you, and, on the other hand, if you learn anything, you must tell me."

"Spoken like your own true self," and Moore fairly beamed on me. "Now, tell me, did she ask you to destroy the book? For of course I only assumed that."

"Yes, she did. Said she was watched or followed and the thing must be absolutely destroyed."

"Then, knowing as we do, what story is in this book, knowing, from Maud, that it is a story of a murder setting forth the very method of Sampson Tracy's murderer, and knowing that Alma Remsen wants this book destroyed secretly, what are we to think?"

"I don't know, I'm sure, what you are to think, but I know that my thoughts include no slightest suspicion of her having done this thing. Accessory after the fact, perhaps. Shielding that man or woman or both, who are there taking care of her, but implicated herself, no!"

"It may well be you are right," Kee said, slowly. "I hope to Heaven it's no worse than that. But it must be investigated. If you were not in love with Alma, if she were not in any way a lovable person, you would be keen to look into these strange facts and circumstances. Now, have you a right to interfere with my pursuance of my duty and my taking up a case which is in line with my profession and my life work? I am influenced by no wrong motive, prejudiced by no personal bias, and as I see it, it is my plain duty to help all I can toward the cause of justice and right. Suspicion rests on many people. Many of these must be innocent. Is it right to let them remain under a cloud, under an unjust doubt, because you have come to love one of the principal actors in this drama?"

"No," I said, desiring most honestly to play fair, "no, but I shall have to work on Alma's side, even if that means working against you."

"That's all right, so long as you work fairly. As you said, tell me all you discover, and listen to all I discover. Then, we are at one, and the truth will conquer. How far have you gone with her? Are you two engaged?"

The calm way he said this brought me to my senses. Of course, we weren't engaged, she hadn't even said she loved me or wanted me to love her. And I told Kee this, and he smiled kindly, and held out his hand.

"Bless you, my children," he said, but with a little catch in his voice.

CHAPTER XIV

POSY MAY

"Well," Keeley began, as we arranged ourselves comfortably on the glass-enclosed porch and prepared for a confab, "our impulsive friend here has gone and done it now!"

The two women gave me a quick look, and Lora, with her uncanny intuition, said:

"When is the wedding, Gray?"

"As soon as it can be arranged," I declared, stoutly, for I wasn't going to be secretive about this matter, anyway. "But don't plan for it yet, Lora, for the lady hasn't by any means said yes. It's only, so far, that 'Barkis is willin'.'"

"It is serious," Keeley said, slowly. "It's all serious, and getting more so every minute. I say, you'll have to excuse me, I've got to go on an errand."

He rose hastily and gathering up his hat and coat, started off down the road.

"Kee's on the warpath for sure," declared Lora. "What happened at Whistling Reeds, Gray?"

"Nothing much—or, yes, I suppose there were developments. Better wait till Kee comes back. He went over the house on a searching bout."

"Did he find anything?"

"I don't know, but I doubt if he found anything as important as I did. You girls may as well know, first as last, I found—that is—I was given—oh, pshaw, here it is—Alma asked me to destroy a book for her, and it was a copy of that book that has in it the story of The Nail."

"No!" cried Maud, aghast at the revelation. "Then——" She paused.

"Now, don't jump at conclusions," Lora begged, looking at me with the utmost kindness, "To find that book there doesn't necessarily point to Alma. It may implicate that old harridan of a nurse or her caveman husband. Far more likely than that cultured girl!"

I looked at her gratefully.

"Good for you, Lora," I said. "Now I'm going to fight this thing to a finish. I'm far from ready to admit that the book's presence at that house is a proof of anything; but of course, it must be investigated. The worst part of it is that Alma asked me secretly to destroy it."

"She would, if she is shielding either of those two caretakers of hers. She is devoted to them, and I for one shouldn't be at all surprised if one or both of them did that murder. You see, they were afraid that the marriage of Mr. Tracy would cut off the fortune from their beloved mistress and so there's motive enough."

"But not a shred of evidence," I said. "And the evidence against Alma is simply piling up. The print of a shoe sole in the window sill shows diamond-shaped dots, as you know, and Alma denied having any other rubber-soled shoes. But, on the garden path there were distinct prints of soles with diamond-shaped dots, and when Kee saw them, he drew my attention. And besides," in my despair I blurted out the whole story, "Alma told me she had destroyed the shoes."

"You poor boy," and that blessed Lora patted my shoulder encouragingly, as she flitted about, "don't put too much weight on those facts. I begin to see through it all. Alma was there, in that room—must have been—but she was not the criminal. Nor did she cut up all those monkey tricks in the bedroom. But these things must be sifted. Keeley will do it, once he gets fairly started. That is, Gray, if you will help him. Do believe me, when I tell you it is far better for you to be frank. Do you know, even now, Kee thinks you're holding out on him."

"I certainly should have held out on that confounded book, if I'd had the least idea he would sneak it away from me! Good Lord, Lora, you've been in love—what would you have done if every man's hand was against Kee and you——"

"Hold on there, Gray, I love Kee now as much as I ever did! And I'm not saying I wouldn't lie or steal for him. But not if I were convinced that honesty was the best plan. No matter what you know or what you may learn against Alma, let Kee in on it, for that is the only way to prove her innocence."

"You haven't any doubt of her innocence, have you, Gray?" Maud asked, gently.

"No, Maudie, I haven't. But there are such blatant, glaring bits of evidence that seem to be against her, that I am afraid others won't be willing to sift them down, but will assume them to be proof positive of her guilt."

"But if she is shielding some one else, as she must be, surely detectives like Keeley and Mr. March will see through it. Mr. March isn't nearly as keen as Keeley, but he's nobody's fool, and he can see through a millstone with a hole in it."

"She tries to take it all so lightly," I went on, thinking aloud.

"Keeley made her say she left her fingerprints when she tried to raise that window, and then he flung at her that it was raining all Tuesday afternoon. And she only said: 'Oh, well, then it must have been Monday.' Now, that's all right, and probably it was Monday, but March won't be satisfied with that. He'll cross question her and bullyrag her until he gets her so mixed up she won't know where she's at!"

"But, Gray," Lora said, quietly, "have you realized that those fingerprints are not such as would be made in an attempt to raise the window? They are on the frame, not on the sash. They are obviously the marks made by some one who stepped up on the window sill and sprang out of the window. Kee is positive about this. He has examined them minutely."

"Then Heaven help Alma," I groaned. "For they say they are her fingerprints and her footprints and she admits that she had that Totem thing in her mind. But it's too clear! It's too obvious! She never killed her uncle, fixed up all that gimcrack business and then went in the sitting room and jumped out of the window!"

"Stick to the things she evidently did do," put in Maud. "She must have stood on the sill and dived out of the window——"

"Not necessarily," I stormed. "Even if she stepped up on the sill, say, to open a window that stuck, that doesn't say she jumped, nor does it prove she killed her uncle."

"Certainly not—hush, somebody is coming up the steps."

The somebody proved to be Posy May, the pretty youngster whom I had seen a few times already.

"Well, how goes it?" she demanded, dropping into a chair and curling her feet under her, while I accommodated her with a cigarette and a light.

"How goes what?" asked Maud, who was not entirely in favour of the young lady, being herself of the type that can't quite understand the flapper motif.

"Oh, the detective business in general. It intrigues me, you know. I sometimes think I'll take a correspondence course in Sherlocking."

"What are you doing to-day?" Lora said, pleasantly. "Why aren't you at the McClellan's tea?"

"Nixie on the switch! I like the subject I started better. And you needn't scorn me so. I could a tale unfold...."

Annoyed beyond measure by this impudent minx, I rose and sauntered toward the house door.

But Lora had evidently caught a note of reality in the girl's voice, for she said, almost sharply, "What do you know, Posy? If you know anything concerning the matter, it is your duty to tell of it."

"I'd rather tell Mr. Moore," she put on an air of importance. "He is at the head of the investigation, I assume."

Lora smiled, in spite of herself, at the chit's manner, but she only said, suavely:

"As a good wife, I am my husband's helpmeet in all his business. And I assure you it will be better to tell me and let me pass it on to him, for he's gone out, and I don't know when he'll get home again."

"Do tell us," Maud urged, helpfully. "We are all intrigued, as you say, with the case, and your assistance might prove invaluable."

The flattering glance that accompanied this speech seemed to win the day, and Posy settled back in the big chair, sticking her feet out straight in front of her.

"Well," she said, smoothing down her brief and scant skirt, "you see, our house is on down the lake, next below Whistling Reeds."

Recognizing there was or might be something coming, I turned back, and sat down again.

"So, of course, I can't help seeing them about now and then, though I don't really rubber much—I don't get time, as I'm busy on my own. And, after all, there's nothing to see, and if there was, you can't see much with all that wall of evergreens all round about."

"If this is idle gossip, my dear——" Lora began.

"No, it's—it's information."

Thoroughly enjoying the attention she was receiving, Posy prolonged the situation by selecting and lighting a fresh cigarette. Having drawn one puff, she turned it round and critically surveyed the lighted end, as is the absurd habit of some people.

But each one of her hearers knew better than to interrupt by word or look the possible continuance of her revelations.

"Now, what I have to tell, I've never breathed to a soul. I'm not sure now that I ought to breathe it."

She looked questioningly about, but we gave no aid or hindrance, knowing the best plan was to let her alone.

Then she drew a long sigh, and let the whole story pour forth in a mad rush of words.

"And it's only one thing I saw, and one thing I heard. And I saw Alma Remsen, out on the tennis court, in a perfectly fiendish rage, and she was striking that old nurse person of hers and calling her the most terrible names, and the man who takes care of the place came and carried her into the house."

"Carried the nurse?"

"No, of course not! Carried Alma into the house, and she was kicking and fighting like mad. And the other time was when I was out on the lake and I could see just the same sort of row going on,

121

but I was too far to hear what she said. But this time the man wasn't about and the nurse managed by herself to drag Alma into the house."

"You're sure what you are saying is true, Posy?" asked Lora, very gravely and with an intent look at the girl.

"Oh, yes, Mrs. Moore, I'm sure, and the reason I'm telling you is because I think that Alma isn't—you know—isn't quite right, sometimes. She isn't—exactly, all there. And then, except on these occasions, she is all right, her own sweet, lovely self."

"Do you know Alma well, Miss Posy?" I asked.

"Oh, yes. We come up here every summer, I've known her for five or six years. She's older than I am, we don't go in the same set, but we meet at fairs and tournaments and she's always most chummy with me. Now, I know you all think I'm telling this just to make a sensation and all that, but it isn't at all. I've thought it over a lot, and it seemed to be my duty. You see, I've doped it out that she has spells—you know, epileptic, or whatever they call it, and that they don't come on often, but when they do, she has no control over her passions. She becomes—oh, somebody else, like—and she fights like a mad person. If you'd seen her go for Mr. Merivale—wow! I don't want to see it again!"

"I can't help thinking you're mistaken in your diagnosis, Miss May," I said, speaking indulgently, for I didn't want her to flare up. "But I think it's far more likely the two occasions you speak of were just fits of anger, unladylike, perhaps, even unjustifiable, but not the result of a diseased mind or body."

She looked at me with earnest eyes.

"You wouldn't say that if you had seen her, Mr. Norris. She was mad—I mean mad, in the sense of demented—I don't mean just angry. Well, anyway, I've told my story, now you can take it up. But I know, if you go there and face that nurse down, she'll have to admit there's some such state of things as I tell you of. She'd deny it to me, or to these ladies, but if a man went there and made her tell the truth, you'd soon find out! That's why she had to be put out of her uncle's house, when he decided to get a wife in there. He couldn't bring a wife to a home with a girl like that in it. If it had not been for his approaching wedding, Mr. Tracy never would have put Alma out."

"Posy," Lora spoke gently, "are you willing to keep this secret a while longer? Are you willing to promise not to tell anybody about it until Mr. Moore says you may? If you will do this, you may feel that you have been of real help to us, but if you're going to spread the story you will do incalculable harm."

"No, I won't tell if you don't want me to."

122

"That's a good girl and we certainly don't want you to. Don't even tell Dick Hardy, will you?"

"Oh, gosh, no! He wouldn't listen, anyway. He's just my sheik, you know. He and I don't talk about anything serious."

"You're a funny youngster, Posy," and Lora smiled kindly at her, "but I'm going to trust your word in this thing. If you say you won't tell, you won't, will you?"

"No, ma'am, I sure won't. And, I don't s'pose you can get me, but I seemed to think the ends of justice couldn't be served unless I coughed up my yarn."

"Oh, Posy, you funny kid!" said Maud, laughing outright.

But Posy didn't smile, nor, indeed, did I.

After a few more words she went off, and as she ran round the corner of the hedge I felt that doubtless she had dismissed the subject from her addle-pated head.

For a few moments we sat, silently thinking over the story we had heard.

I broke the silence finally by saying, "It's too circumstantial not to be true."

"Yes," Lora agreed, "it's true, right enough, but I can't quite understand."

"Nothing hard to understand," I argued. "Alma has a more uncontrollable temper than I had any idea of. This doesn't make me think she went so far as to kill her uncle in one of her angry fits but I will say that the matter must be looked into."

"Kee will look into it," Lora said, with one of her gentle smiles.

Kee's wife was a good sort, and she always tried to make things easy and pleasant for me. I knew, though, that she was thinking over this thing, and I dreaded to learn whither her thoughts led her.

For I distinctly remembered Mrs. Dallas saying that Sampson Tracy had wanted to tell her something about Alma, something unpleasant, she had implied. What could it have been but this, that the girl had, at times, an ungovernable temper?

For I was determined I would not believe that the trouble lay deeper than that. That the sweet girl I adored had a flaw in her brain or a physical disorder that meant impaired intellect in any way!

We ignored the subject by common consent, Lora, no doubt feeling that since it must be discussed with Kee, there was small use mulling it over beforehand.

And then, Kee returned.

He was full of some news of his own, so we listened to him first.

"It's about that sound Ames heard," he told us. "You know he said, after several false starts, that it was like a stick drawn along a wall.

"Well, it occurred to me that, if it was anything at all, it might be the murderer trailing along, with his hammer and nail in his hand, and if the hall was dark, feeling along the walls and doors to guide him."

"Rather far-fetched." I smiled.

"Well, the only way to see about it was to look on the door of Ames's room and there, sure enough, was a long scratch, as if a nail or something had been dragged along it. A distinct scratch, but only across the door—at least, I could find no other such mark. So, me for the Coroner's office to look over the exhibits. And, if you please, with a powerful lens, I discovered some minute particles of dark varnish in under the head of that nail that played the principal part in our death drama."

"Seems incredible," I murmured, and indeed it did.

"Yes, but true," Kee averred. "And the brown varnish corresponds exactly to the door of Ames's room, all the doors in that wing, in fact."

"Well, after all, what does it prove?" I asked, wearily, wondering what new horror was to be divulged.

"Only premeditation. It proves that the murderer went to Tracy's room, passing by Ames's room, carrying the nail with him, and presumably the hammer. That's all I can see in it, but it lends a bit of colour to Maud's idea that the story of The Nail may have been responsible for the whole thing."

"Yes," I said, holding myself together, "it does. But of course, even though we found that book at the house on the Island, there are several inmates of that house who may become suspect; also there is the possibility that one of those inmates may have lent that book to anybody in all Deep Lake."

"Perfectly true, Gray," and Keeley spoke almost casually. "That's logical enough. Now to find out who did or might have done that. It's quite on the cards that somebody in the Pleasure Dome household read that book and used that method to do away with Tracy. It's even possible that a rank outsider did the same thing. But somebody did do it, and with that book in the vicinity it's only rational to assume the connection between the suggestion and the deed."

"Could it have been the work of a demented person?" asked Maud.

"Very easily," Keeley said. "I've hoped all along some maniac would turn up whom we could suspect. But none has, so far. Yes, it all has the earmarks of the work of a distorted brain, I mean the feather duster and all that tomfoolery. But I've not been able to find any trace of anybody even slightly or temporarily demented."

Well, then, of course, Posy May's story had to be told to him.

Lora undertook the telling, and without any help from Maud or me, she gave a clear and concise résumé of Posy's statements.

Kee listened, as always, thoughtfully and with deepest interest.

When she had finished, he turned to me and said, in what was intended for a comforting manner:

"Take it easy, old man. The game's never out till it's played out. I'm not at all of the opinion that the scenes the volatile Posy described actually happened just as she described them. It may be Alma lost her temper, lost it to such an extent that the Merivales, one and all, urged her into the house. But make allowances for the source of that information and remember that it may all have happened some time ago, that Posy's memory may be greatly stimulated by her imagination, and that she is decidedly prone to exaggerate, anyway."

My very drooping spirits revived and I plucked up a little hope. But I had to know what Kee thought about the book.

"Do you feel sure, as Maud does, that the story in the book started the whole thing?"

"As I said, a few moments ago, I do, at this moment, think there is some connection, but I am quite willing to say, also, that it is, to my mind, just as likely there is none."

"Then why did Alma want the book destroyed?" I demanded.

"Because she thinks there is a connection——"

My heart lightened.

"That," I exclaimed, "proves you think her innocent."

"I never said I didn't think that. But thinking so is a far cry from proving it. If you, Gray, could only bring yourself to tell me the important bit of information you are holding out on me, I should know better where we stand. I think, boy, the time has come—if you're ever going to tell—to tell now."

I pondered. How could I tell them that I had seen Alma on the lake that night? How could I put her dear head in the noose?—for it was nothing less than that. I shook my head.

"There's nothing, Kee," I said.

"Don't tell, if you don't want to, Gray, but don't think you can lie to me successfully. You can't."

"But, Keeley," I begged him, "granting I do know of a point that I haven't told you, and supposing it definitely incriminates the girl I love, can you wonder that I want to withhold it?"

"You mean you think it definitely incriminates her. You may well be mistaken."

"It doesn't seem so to me."

"And you propose to lock this important piece of information in your own soul, away from us all, and let us go on, blindly floundering——"

"Do you suppose I care how blindly you flounder if you don't suspect Alma Remsen? Do you suppose I care that I'm accessory after the fact, and all that, if I can keep her safe from suspicion?"

"But, Gray, if I can convince you that it's wiser to let me know, and if I promise not to utilize the information you give me, if it does prove her guilty, what then?"

"If you give me your word of honour on that, I'll tell."

"Very well, word of honour."

"Then," I said, "I saw Alma Remsen in her canoe go to Pleasure Dome at about half-past one that night her uncle died, and I saw—no, I heard, her come back past here about half-past two."

"How are you so sure of this?" Kee asked. "You didn't know her then. That was the very night you arrived here."

"I know that. I was looking out of my bedroom window and saw the girl; it was moonlight and I saw her distinctly. Then, next day when I saw Alma I recognized her for the same girl."

"And you didn't see her return?"

"I heard her, but I was sleepy and didn't get up to look out. It may not have been she, of course, but it was a sound as of similar paddling."

"I'm glad you told me," Keeley said, but his face was sombre and his eyes sad.

CHAPTER XV

JENNIE

Keeley Moore had a knack of putting his troubles away on a high shelf, while he relaxed, as he called it. And with him, this meant relaxation of mind as well as body, and he stretched himself in his porch chair, and demanded light chatter, with no hint or mention of the Pleasure Dome tragedy.

Lora, as usual, met him more than half way, and began a recital of the blunders made by her new parlour maid that morning.

"Nice looking little baggage," said Kee, who had always an eye for a pretty face. "Where'd you pick her up?"

"I can't tell you that," said Lora, "it's a secret."

"A secret? Where you got a servant! Then, I can guess; you sneaked her away from some unsuspecting friend, and offered higher wages."

"Nothing of the sort! Jennie came to me and asked me to take her."

"Where has she been living?"

"Oh, nowhere in particular. How do you like that screen across that corner? It was in the dining room, you know, but it wasn't really necessary there——"

"Hush, woman!" thundered Kee, in mock rage. "Don't trifle with me. Tell me where that parlour maid sprang from, or tremble for your life!"

"But I can't," and Lora broke into giggles. "You see, you've forbidden me to tell you——"

"Forbidden you to tell me!" Kee sat up, his keen intuition telling him there was something back of this chaffing.

"Yes. To tell you would involve the mention of a forbidden name——"

"Lora! You've taken on a servant from Pleasure Dome!"

"Yes. I couldn't resist. She's a jewel, and she had already left there."

"She was free to come?"

"Oh, yes. Griscom has dismissed several of the maids, saying there's not enough work for a large force."

"The household is as it was except for Mr. Tracy."

"Yes, of course, but there's no entertaining, and I believe Mr. Ames and young Dean are leaving soon after the funeral."

"Who'll be head of the house, then? Everett, I suppose."

"Kee, you forbade all reference to Pleasure Dome and now you're——"

"Go away, we're not talking of the murder now. A fellow can gossip about his neighbours, I suppose."

"Oh, yes; all right, then. Well, Jennie told me all this, and she says that when Miss Alma comes to live in the big house, she will go back there, if Alma will take her. But she won't stay there now, because Mrs. Fenn is too bossy."

"Mrs. Fenn?"

"Yes, the housekeeper. She and Griscom rule the roost, and the other servants are all squirming."

"Perhaps we can worm some information out of the perspicacious Jennie."

"Keeley Moore! You wouldn't descend to quizzing servants, would you?"

"Wouldn't I just! I'd quiz a scullery maid, if I could get a glimmer of light on our dark problem. Pull Jennie in and let me take a shot at her."

Obediently, Lora touched a bell and Jennie appeared.

She was a trim, tidy young person, in a neat uniform, and her attitude was perfect.

She stood at attention and awaited orders.

Kee looked at her, and then said, slowly, "You have been living at Mr. Tracy's?"

"Yes, sir." The reply was calm, respectful and quite unperturbed.

"Why did you leave there?"

"The butler and housekeeper decided to reduce the staff, and I asked that I might be one of those to leave."

Kee studied her more closely. Clearly, she was superior to the general run of servants.

"Why did you wish to leave?"

She hesitated a moment, then said, in a straightforward manner:

"Because I prefer to work in a house where there is a master or mistress and not a house run by the upper servants."

"That's plausible. Is that the only reason you wanted to make a change?"

A longer pause this time. Then, again, that sudden decision to speak.

"No, sir. I wanted to get away from a house where such a terrible thing had happened."

"That's a natural feeling, I'm sure. You were there, then, at the time of Mr. Tracy's death?"

"Oh, yes."

"Were you questioned by the Coroner about it?"

"No, sir. I suppose he thought I didn't know anything about it."

"And do you?"

"Oh, yes, sir."

Keeley stared at her. I went limp and faint all over and the two women nearly fell off their chairs.

But Kee was careful not to show his intense interest.

"Well, Jennie," he said, in as casual a tone as he could command, "what do you know?"

"Do I have to tell you, sir?"

She looked at him serenely, not at all frightened, and with no diminution of her respectful attitude.

"Why,—er—yes, Jennie, I think you do."

"I mean, legally, you know. Am I bound to answer your questions? Are you a policeman?"

"Why, yes, in a way," Kee began, and then he said, quickly, "no, Jennie, I'm not a policeman, but if you don't tell me, you'll have to tell the police. Now, wouldn't you rather tell me, nice and quietly, than to be interviewed by the police, who would scare you out of your wits?"

"Oh, sir, they couldn't scare me," the girl returned, with a look of self-reliance that seemed to exhibit neither fear of God nor regard of man. I had never seen on the face of one so young such apparent certainty of an ability to hold her own.

Clearly, Jennie was a find, and would doubtless prove a strong card, for, of course, Kee would get her story out of her.

But he soon found that he could not do it himself. Unless convinced that she was forced to it by the law, Jennie had no intention of divulging her information.

Recognizing this, Kee gave it up and sent her about her business.

"She probably knows nothing," was his comment. "If she did, Griscom or Hart would have caught on. I suppose she thought she saw something and her imagination exaggerated it."

"But she doesn't seem to me imaginative, Kee," Lora declared. "Not like Posy, you know, out to kick up a sensation. This girl is queer, very queer, but to me she rings true."

"We'll hear her story before we decide," Kee told her. "March will be over to-night, and he'll have the law on her! Don't let her go out this evening."

Lora agreed and then we went out to dinner. Serious conversation at table was strictly taboo, so we had only light chat and banter throughout the meal.

But afterward, snugly settled in the lounge, Keeley said:

"Well, of course, we have to face facts. There's no use denying, Gray, that matters begin to look pretty thick for Alma. As you know I have to push on; I can't stop because the girl my friend cares for is under suspicion. So, it comes down to this. If you choose, you may go back to New York till it's all over, one way or another. You can't be of any help to me here, and I can't see how you can be of any use to Alma. This sounds a bit brutal, but I think you understand. If you don't, I'll try to explain."

"You'd better explain, then," I growled, "for I'm damned if I do understand."

"Well, it's only that, as I said, you can't help any, and if things go against the girl, it would be better for you to be out of it all."

I suppose something in the look of misery that came into my eyes went to Lora's heart, for she said:

"Nonsense, Kee, Gray can't go away. He couldn't bring himself to do that. Of course, he'll stay right here with us, and if he doesn't help, at least he won't hinder. You go ahead with your investigations and Gray and I will stand at thy right hand and keep the bridge with thee."

"All right, Lora," I managed to say, and Kee understandingly refrained from any further words on the subject.

But I grasped his meaning, and I knew that I was to stay only if I put no obstacles in his way and concealed no information that I might in any way achieve.

March came along as per schedule, and he and Keeley plunged at once into the discussion. Keeley Moore was not one of those private investigators who kept secret his own findings or ideas. He was almost always ready to tell freely what he thought or suspected, and he expected equal frankness from his fellow workers.

So, first of all he informed March of the story Posy May had detailed.

March, too, was inclined to take it with a grain of salt.

"I know that kid," he said. "She's full of the old Nick, and I'm not sure her word is reliable. But that yarn sounds plausible, and if she did see what she describes, it's likely somebody else at some time or other has seen the same sort of thing. If so, I'll try to find it out, and if we get one or two corroborations, we can begin to think it may be so."

"But, even then," I suggested, "it may only mean a high temper and not a—a——"

"A diseased mind," March supplied. "I don't know about that. If it were a case of high temper there would be more or less exhibition of it right along. A girl who flies into wild passions at times is going

130

to have slight shows of temper in between or else there's something radically wrong there. And as I know Miss Remsen, I only know her as a lovely, gentle-natured girl, without this fierce temper at all. If, then, she has spells of it, those spells mean organic trouble of some sort. We could ask her nurse, but we'd learn nothing from her, I'm sure. We could quiz the Pleasure Dome servants, for the older ones, at least, lived there when Alma was there. But again, they would shield her from any suspicion. Or they probably would. We can try it on."

"What about her doctor?" said Lora. "He'd know."

"Yes; and that's a good idea. But her doctor, I think, is Doctor Rogers, and he went to California the day after Mr. Tracy died. He seems to be beyond reach, for he went by the Canadian Pacific, and stopped along the way at various places."

"Banff and Lake Louise, I suppose," suggested Maud.

"Yes, but also at some less known places, ranches or such, and his office says he will get no mail until he reaches San Francisco."

"Fine way for a doctor to leave his arrangements," exclaimed Keeley.

"Oh, well, he put his practice in good hands, and he's gone off for a real vacation. But all he could tell us is whether Alma Remsen is in any way or in any degree mentally affected. And I'm quite sure we can somehow find that out without him. If I grill that old butler and that sphinx of a housekeeper over there, I'm sure I can gather from what they say or don't say about how matters stand."

"If she is epileptic," Maud said, "would it explain a criminal act on her part?"

"It might," March returned, "but I don't think she is that."

"I don't, either," Kee agreed, and I blessed them both silently for that ray of hope.

Then Keeley told of the new parlour maid and her strange attitudes, and March demanded her immediate presence.

"A servant from that house is just what we want," he said. "We are in luck."

Jennie answered Lora's summons, and appeared, looking as composed and serene as before.

Clearly she had no intention of quailing before the majesty of the law.

"You may sit down, Jennie," Lora said, kindly, and the girl took a chair with just the right shade of deference and obedience.

"You were employed at Pleasure Dome?" March began, a trifle disconcerted at this self-possessed young creature.

"Yes, sir."

"For how long?"

131

"I was there six months."

"Then you were there when Mr. Tracy died?"

"Yes, sir."

"But you were not there when Miss Remsen lived there?"

"No, sir."

"No. Now, Jennie, you told Mrs. Moore you knew something about the night of Mr. Tracy's death."

"Yes, sir."

"Is it, do you think, of importance?"

"Yes, sir."

Not only the monotony of the girl's monosyllabic replies, but the enigmatic smile that played about her lips and was remindful of the Mona Lisa, began to grate on the nerves of all of us.

But March swallowed, took a long breath, and plunged into the matter.

"Then, Jennie, since you deem it of importance, tell it to us, and we will see what we think about it."

"Must I tell it, sir?"

"Indeed you must," and March glared at her threateningly.

But it was unnecessary. Jennie seemed to think it a case of needs must when the law drives, and she began to speak in real sentences.

"You see," she said, "my room is across the house from Mr. Tracy's room. I mean across the part of Deep Lake that he called the Sunless Sea."

"Across?"

"Yes, sir. You can look out of my window and see down into Mr. Tracy's room. Of course, my room is on the third floor and his on the second, but you can see in."

"Yes, and did you see in?"

"Oh, yes, I often looked in there late at night."

"What for?"

"Nothing in particular, only it was bright and gay and there were always flowers about, and sometimes company and music, and so I liked to look at it."

"Well, go on."

"Yes, sir. And never did I see anything strange or peculiar, except this one night, sir. You see, it was his sitting room as I could look into, and it was so fixed, with curtains and all that, that I couldn't really see much after all. I just sort of had a glimpse like, and then nothing."

"I see. Well, get along to the night of the strange thing you saw. What was it?"

"I saw Miss Alma dive out of the window into the lake."

There was a moment's dead silence and then March found his voice somehow, and carried on.

"You're—you're sure it was Miss Remsen?"

"Oh, yes, sir, of course. I know her well."

"How was she dressed?"

"She had on a white dress, a sports suit, and white shoes and stockings. She most always wears white in the summer time. She came to the window, and I saw her step up on the sill, and then she looked down at the lake for a moment."

"As if afraid?"

"Oh, no, sir. As if just judging the distance, or something like that, Then, she put her hands together over her head, and dived right off. She went down like a lovely bird, into the water and in a few seconds up again, and straight out to where her boat was, near by."

"What sort of boat?"

"The little canoe she always uses, sir. I know it well."

"And then?"

"Then, sir, she settled herself in the boat, all dripping wet as she was, but she didn't seem to mind, and she paddled away just as she always paddled, with that clear, sharp stroke that everybody admires so much."

"Where did she go?"

"Toward her own home, on the Island. Of course, when she turned the bend I couldn't see her."

"What did you do then?"

"I went to bed, sir."

"Put out your light?"

"I didn't have any light. It was moonlight and I was just looking out at the lake when this thing happened."

"Jennie, this is a very strange tale."

"Yes, sir."

"You say it is true—all of it?"

"Every word, sir."

The girl's eyes were of a dull gray, but they had a penetrating gaze that was a bit irritating.

But both eyes and voice carried conviction.

None of Jennie's listeners was the kind to be hoodwinked, and moreover we all rather fancied ourselves as being able to discern between true and false witnessing.

And as we found later, when we compared notes, each of us was thoroughly impressed with the indubitable truthfulness of this strange girl with her strange story.

"And you've not told this before?"

"No, sir."

"Why not?"

"I wasn't asked."

"Who asked you now?"

"Mrs. Moore, sir, and then Mr. Moore, and then yourself."

"Yes, I see. Well, Jennie, can you keep this story secret for a time?"

"If nobody asks me about it."

"But look here, girl, you are in the command of the law, and I order you not to tell this. You're bound to obey me, or you will be put in prison. See, in prison!"

"I shouldn't like that, sir."

But even this avowal brought no change of countenance or gleam of fear to the gray eyes.

"You bet you wouldn't. But that's what you'll get if you tell."

"Yes, sir."

"Will you keep still about it?"

"If nobody asks me, sir."

March looked utterly disgusted, but Lora took the matter in hand.

"Leave it to me, Mr. March," she said. "I think I can answer for Jennie's obedience to your order so long as she stays with me."

"I like you," said Jennie, gazing at her.

"Of course you do," said Lora, heartily, "and I like you. We're going to be great friends. Now, Mr. March, any more questions before I put our star witness to bed?"

"A few only. Jennie, did you see Miss Remsen come to the house, or only go away?"

"Only go away."

"Do you suppose she came to the house in her boat?"

"She must have done so, she always comes that way. But she could not have gone in by the window."

"No. How did she get in, then?"

"By the door, I suppose. Miss Remsen had a key."

"Then, why did she leave by the window?"

"That's what I don't know," the gray eyes clouded. "That's what I can't make out."

"It is a hard problem. What time was it when you saw her go away?"

"I've no idea. We all go to bed at ten, if it isn't our night out. So I went to my room about ten, but I couldn't sleep."

"Hadn't you been asleep at all, when you saw the girl and the boat?"

134

"Yes, I think so. I'm quite sure I had. But my watch wasn't going, and so I don't know what time it was."

"Don't you have a timepiece to get up by?"

"Mrs. Fenn raps on our doors, sir, then we get up."

"I see. Well, you say it was moonlight. Do you know where the moon was, in the sky?"

"Oh, yes, it was just disappearing behind Mr. Tracy's wing."

"Then we can track the time down by that," said March, with a nod of satisfaction. "Given the date and the position of the moon, that's easy."

"Jennie," said Keeley, thoughtfully, "did Miss Remsen have anything in her hands when she dived from the window?"

"Oh, I forgot to tell you that. You see, her canoe was just below, right down from the window. She leaned out first, and dropped a bundle of something into the boat. Then, she stepped on the sill, and I could see she did have something in one hand. A sort of stick, I think."

"The Totem Pole," said March, decidedly.

"That's all, Jennie, you may go now."

Lora left the room with the girl, but soon returned, Not a word had been spoken by us in her absence.

"Well," she said, as she came back, and March responded, "not well at all. About as bad as it can be."

"You believe that balderdash, then?" I asked, angrily, and Keeley said, "Yes, Gray, and so do you. I think, March, we must revert to the mentally deficient theory."

"I think so, too," March said, shaking his head. "I wish Doctor Rogers was at home."

135

CHAPTER XVI

WHISTLING REEDS

March called in at Variable Winds on his way to the Tracy funeral. We were all ready to go, for though none of us wanted to, it was a matter of convention and the whole village would have commented unkindly had we stayed away.

I, especially, dreaded it, for I dislike funerals, and I hated the thought of the entire community sitting up there, casting glances at Alma and making whispered remarks about her.

But I had to go, so I made the best of it, and, garbed in appropriate black, I sat with the others awaiting the time to start.

March came in, looking harassed and worn.

"It's all too dreadful," he said, sinking into a chair. "Everything seems to point to Alma Remsen, yet I am not convinced of her guilt."

I started to speak, but thought better of it. Since March held that opinion nothing I could say would help any. I'd better keep still.

"I'm going to the funeral," March went on, "because it's wiser to show myself there. But I shall slip out, during the service, and go over to the island house. How about going with me, Mr. Norris?"

"What for?" I asked, a little suspicious of his motives.

"Partly to help along by corroborating anything I may learn or discover and partly that you may tell Mr. Moore all about it later, and save me that much work. I've none too much time for what I have to do."

"Go ahead, Gray," Keeley said. "I can't leave the funeral, of course, but your absence will not be noticed. As neighbours, we must show proper respect, but our guests may be excused."

"Very well, then, I'll go," I told March. For I felt I'd rather know exactly what he found out and so know what steps to take myself.

I was formulating in my mind a course of procedure that I hoped might free Alma from these monstrous and false suspicions.

"I'll go," I repeated, "but not because I foresee any new evidence against Miss Remsen. It's too absurd to suspect her."

"It's too absurd not to," March said. "The evidence is piling up. The fingerprints and footsteps and the maid's story of seeing her that night all seem to prove she was there at the fatal hour. The strange decorations on the deathbed look like the work of a diseased mind. Posy May's story seems to prove that Miss Remsen is afflicted with some sort of spells that transform her into a demoniac. Then, add the details of the waistcoats and Totem Pole, the fact that she is an expert swimmer and the strong motive of the approaching loss of her uncle's fortune——"

"You're going too fast, Mr. March," I interrupted him. "Posy May's story should not be taken without some outside corroboration. She is an irresponsible child, and not fit to be a real witness. The maid, Jennie, I think, comes in the same category. I, for one, am unwilling to admit Miss Remsen the victim of any sort of malady or disease until we have a doctor's opinion on that subject. It seems to me this is only fair to the young lady."

"Norris is right about that," Keeley agreed with me. "Keep these developments quiet for another twenty-four hours, March. No good can come from exploiting them."

"No, and I don't mean to. But no harm can come of going over to the Remsen house, even if it does no good."

"All right as to that. Go ahead. Go with him, Gray, and keep your eyes and ears open. The two Merivales will probably be at the funeral, but there'll doubtless be some one in charge of the place."

It was time to start then, and we walked sedately out to the car, our funeral manner already upon us.

The two Moores and Maud went up toward the front seats, while March and I took seats in the back of the room.

The services were held at Pleasure Dome, in the great ballroom that was beneath the rooms of Sampson Tracy's suite.

I looked out the window at the deep, dark lake. Sunless Sea was an apt name for it, as the trees grew thickly right down to the very edge of the water, and the great house also shaded it. A sombre-looking scene, yet of a certain still peacefulness that had its own appeal.

Here and there a rock lifted its jagged form up out of the water, but I realized that if a diver or swimmer were familiar with the place, he could easily avoid danger.

My heart was sick at the black clouds that seemed to be closing in round the girl I loved, and I resolved anew to devote my whole heart and soul to the task of setting her free.

I had no doubt of her innocence, no doubt but that these seemingly true counts against her were really capable of some other explanation, but even if she were guilty, even if she had killed her uncle, whether in her right mind or not, she was still the one girl in the world for me. I would comfort and help her in her adversity as I would in more joyful hours, should such ever come to us.

Then I saw her come in—saw Alma enter, her arm through that of the faithful Merry, while John Merivale stalked behind them like a bodyguard.

What a pair those Merivales were! Invincible seemed to be the only word that described them. Strong, brave, keen-witted, they looked forceful and capable enough to ward off all trouble from the girl they loved. But whether they could do so or not was the question.

Alma, white-faced but composed, walked with a steady step, and took the seat the usher offered, in the front row, her faithful henchmen on either side.

Mrs. Dallas was also in the front row, and the secretaries and Harper Ames.

In the next row sat the entire staff of the Pleasure Dome servants. Then came the neighbours and villagers. The room was quickly filled and many were turned away or relegated to other rooms in the house.

The air was heavy with the scent of hothouse flowers, for the well-meaning donors were not content to send the lovely garden flowers blooming on their own estates.

Exquisite music sounded from behind a screen of tall palms, and as the services began, March looked at me, and we silently rose and went out.

"Horrible affairs, funerals," I said, wiping my brow with my handkerchief.

"Oh, I don't know," the detective responded, "I rather like them. I like that exotic effect of the flowers and music and the solemn-faced audience, and the still peaceful figure in the casket. Yes, it impresses me rather pleasantly."

"Then you're a ghoul," I told him, irritably, which was unjust on the face of it.

The good-natured chap only smiled, for he realized, I think, that my nerves were on edge.

"I don't know you very well, Mr. Norris," he said, after a pause, "but I'm going to venture on a bit of advice. I know, of course, your regard for Miss Remsen, and I'm going to warn you that you may hinder rather than help her cause, unless you learn to control your feelings. Don't lose your temper when you see us detectives prying into matters that seem to you sacred. These things must be done. Your objections have no weight, and it is far wiser not to raise them. Maybe I am offending you, but my intentions are good, and you can take it or leave it."

The man's honest countenance and kindly smile affected me more pleasantly than his words, and after a moment I said, heartily:

"I take it, Mr. March. I realize I am a blundering ass, and I'm grateful for a pull-up. But, to be frank, I never was in love before, and to find suddenly that I care for a woman with all my heart and soul, and then find her under a terrible suspicion—well, I daresay you'll admit it is a hard position."

"I do. Indeed, I do. And you mustn't give up hope yet. I always keep an open mind just as long as possible. It may be some other claimant for the honour of being the criminal will turn up. I surely hope so. But in the meantime we must just dig into things and do all we can to get more light."

"You're going to search the house on the Island?"

"I certainly am, if I can get in any way. Maybe there's no one there."

"Then you'd break in, I suppose."

"Maybe, maybe. I'd do anything to learn a few things I want to know."

We had reached the Pleasure Dome boathouse now, and from an attendant there March commandeered a small boat, which he said he would row himself.

"I like a bit of exercise," he told me, "and rowing is my preference."

So we went on, past Variable Winds, on down to the Island of Whistling Reeds.

A quiet, rather grim-faced man helped us to make our landing and we went up to the house.

Before we reached it, March paused to give it a moment's study.

We looked at its pleasant porches and its windows with light, fluttering curtains. From one window, on the second floor, a face looked out at us, a girl's face, with dark, bobbed hair.

The head was quickly withdrawn, and we went up the steps and March rang the bell.

In a moment the door was opened by the girl whose face we had seen at the window. She now wore a bit of a frilled cap with a black velvet bow.

This she had obviously donned at the sound of the doorbell.

"We have come," March said to her, in his pleasant way, "to look over the house."

"It isn't for sale," she said, not frightened at all, but seeming a little amused.

"I know. I don't want to buy or rent it. Are you the parlour maid?"

"I'm Miss Remsen's personal maid—lady's maid," she returned, bridling a bit, as if to be a parlour maid was beneath her rank.

"Oh, I see. I thought Miss Remsen had her nurse——"

"Yes. Mrs. Merivale is my mother. We both look after Miss Alma."

"I'm sure she's well taken care of. Now——"

"Dora, sir," she said, divining his question with quick intuition.

"Well, Dora, I suppose you are devoted to Miss Remsen?"

"Oh, that I am, sir. I'd die for her!"

"Well, we don't want you to do that, but something far easier. We just want you to answer a few questions. Is anybody in the house beside yourself?"

"Nobody, sir."

"All gone to the funeral?"

"Yes, sir. All but Michael, down at the dock, and me."

"Very well. Now, do you remember the night Mr. Tracy died?"

"Yes, sir."

"Where was Miss Remsen that night?"

"Here at home, sir."

"What did she do through the evening?"

"She read in a book, sir, then she played the piano a bit and then she went to bed."

This was reeled off glibly, a little too glibly, I thought. It sounded parrot-like, as if a lesson, learned by rote. Evidently March thought so too, for he said, looking at her closely:

"How do you know this?"

"How do I know?" she looked a little blank. "Oh, yes, I know, because I saw her now and again as I passed through the hall."

"I see. Now, what book was she reading? Do you know?"

"No, sir, I don't know that."

"But you saw her reading?"

"Yes, sir."

"Well, what kind of book was it? A big book?"

"No—no, sir, I think not. I think it was a smallish book——"

"With a paper cover?"

"Yes, sir, with a paper cover."

"Stop it, March," I cried, involuntarily. "You sha'n't put words into her mouth!"

"Keep still, Norris," he said, sternly, "and remember what I told you."

I supposed he meant that I could serve Alma best by learning everything possible about her, but I resented this sort of procedure.

The girl was frightened, too. She drew her breath quickly, as if fearing she had been indiscreet, but March restored her equanimity by his next words.

"That's all right, Dora," he said, "it doesn't matter what book she had or what music she played. Then she went to bed? She didn't go out anywhere?"

"Oh, no, sir, it was near ten, then. Miss Remsen never goes out evenings unless to a party and then somebody fetches her or Mother goes with her."

"Well, you've told a straight story, and that's all we want to know. Now, I'm going to give the house the once over."

"What's that, sir?"

"A glance about. You see, Dora, I'm connected with the police and——"

"The police, sir!" she cried, and sank into a chair.

But suddenly she sprang to her feet again, and said, in a low, tense tone, "Will you please go away, sir? Go away, and come when my father or mother shall be here?"

"No, Dora, we can't do that. You ought to know that the police cannot be told what to do. But rest assured, we mean no harm to your young mistress, and we are hoping to find some clues or evidence that will free her from suspicion."

Dora looked thoroughly perplexed. She glanced from the window, as if of a mind to call Michael, but he was not in sight.

"And I may as well tell you," March continued, his iron hand still in a velvet glove, "that you'd better let us have our way, without raising any objection. For you can't stop us, and you'd only create unpleasantness for yourself."

Dora seemed to see reason, and she nodded her head in assent.

"What do you want me to do?" she asked, in a subdued voice.

"Go with us and show us the rooms. That's all. We shall not really disturb anything and it will save Miss Remsen trouble if we can get through before her return."

So Dora went ahead, with an air of obedience under protest that showed itself in her dragging footsteps and her sombre eyes.

"This is the living room," she said, indicating the room we already knew.

March stepped inside. He quickly scanned the appointments, but he had seen them before and paid real attention only to the bookcase. This produced nothing of interest, however, and we went on through a cozy little writing room to the dining room, a delightful cheery room hung with chintzes and gay with bowls of flowers.

To my amazement, the detective devoted his scrutiny to the dining table. He examined the wood of it carefully and then drawing a lens from his pocket peered through it in true Sherlock Holmes fashion.

I wondered if this was meant to impress the staring Dora, but March seemed to be interested on his own account, and he pocketed his lens with a sigh of satisfaction.

"Now the kitchen," he said, and we went thither.

141

A modern, immaculate kitchen it was, with all the up-to-date contrivances for lightening labour and for achieving quick results.

March took in most of it at a glance, pausing only to turn round a can of cocoa on a shelf in the glass-doored cupboard.

"Yes," he said, smiling at Dora, "I think that's the best brand, too."

Then we went upstairs.

It seemed sacrilege to me to go into Alma's bedroom, but March strode forward as a general to an attack.

He made no noise or disturbance, he opened no cupboards or bureau drawers. He looked closely at the bedside table, which showed only a reading lamp, a book or two, a small flask of cologne water and an engagement pad and pencil.

"Miss Alma has her breakfast in bed," he said, interrogatively, and I wondered if he had seen a spot on the lace table cover, or how he knew.

"Yes, sir. Both—both Sundays and weekdays, sir."

Dora was blushing furiously now, though I could see no reason for it at mere mention of breakfast in bed.

March seemed not to see it, and went on to the next room. This was a large and delightful room, the counterpart of Alma's bedroom.

"The guest room," Dora said, and stood aside to let us enter.

"And a pretty one. Are there guests often?"

"Oh, yes, sir. Miss Alma frequently has young ladies to stay the night with her."

"I see. A charming room." He set down his stick, while he leaned out of the window for a glimpse of the lake.

He looked into the guest bathroom, but it showed only the immaculate cleanliness beloved of all good housekeepers, and then we went back into the hall.

"Where are the servants' rooms?" he asked.

"Up in the third story, sir. Want to go up?"

Dora opened a door at the foot of a flight of stairs, but March said, "No, not necessary," and she closed it again.

"Now, we'll go downstairs," he said, and we started. He let Dora precede and then pushed me along next.

Exclaiming, "Oh, I've left my stick!" he returned to the guest room, and came out again, carrying the stick in question.

I felt sure the stick was a blind of some sort, but I couldn't see how he had found any clue in the guest room, and I was weary of the farce anyway.

What did he expect to find? As far as I could see, he hadn't found anything at all.

"Well, Dora," he said, as we regained the porch, and were about

142

to leave. "You've been very kind. You can tell Miss Remsen and your parents all about it, and tell them you behaved just exactly right."

"Yes, sir. Thank you, sir."

"Has Miss Remsen a beau?"

"She's not engaged, sir, but several young men are sweet on her."

"Who?" I cried, feeling that I'd like to knock the several heads together.

"I think Mr. Billy Dean is the nicest," Dora said, apparently quite willing to gossip.

"Miss Remsen is never ill, is she?" March broke in.

"Oh, no, sir, never."

"Never has to take anything to induce sleep?"

"Oh, n' no—never." But this time there was hesitation, and I pictured Alma as unable to sleep and resorting to a mild sedative.

"All right, Dora, good-bye, and many thanks."

We went down to the boathouse, and the man there was still glum and unsmiling. Nor did our substantial douceur give him any apparent pleasure. He pocketed it without a word, and pushed off our boat with a jerk that had the effect of his being glad to be rid of us.

March was unperturbed by all this and of course it mattered little to me.

I was consumed with curiosity to know if March had learned anything indicative.

"I found a few trifles," he vouchsafed to tell me, "but I can't describe them at the moment."

"Being a detective, you have to be mysterious," I growled.

"Yes, just that," he agreed, cheerfully, and we proceeded in silence. "They're just leaving the burying ground," he said, at last. "Shall we go and pay our final respects?"

"If you like," I said, indifferently.

So we landed at Pleasure Dome, and then betook ourselves to the tiny graveyard, which was down beyond the orchard.

It was a lovely spot, shaded by the long branches of weeping willows and brightened by beds of carefully tended flowers. Lilies abounded, and there were patches of the lovely California poppies and screens covered with sweet peas.

I became interested in the graves, and March pointed out those of Alma's parents and her little sister.

"The child was eight years old when she died," I commented. "I thought it was an infant."

"No, a girl. Alma remembers her, of course. But it was all before my day. I've only lived here seven years. Flowers enough on Tracy's grave, in all conscience."

The mound of the new grave was heaped with flowers, indeed an impressive sight. The growing flowers and the cut blossoms vied with each other in beauty, and harmonized into one glorious whole of gorgeous bloom.

All had left but two or three workmen, and they withdrew to a respectful distance while March and I stood there.

"Tell me, March, did you find anything? I can't bear this suspense!"

"Please believe I don't want to keep you on tenterhooks," he said, with real regret in his tone. "But what I did discover is so contradictory, so impossible of solution, at present, that I can't divulge it until I find some meaning to it. What did you make of the girl, Dora?"

"Nothing. She seemed to me just an ordinary servant——"

"Don't you believe it! She's far from being an ordinary servant! That girl knows all there is to know."

"What do you mean?"

"Just what I say. And we've got to get that knowledge."

"Of course, then, if she knows anything, it's to do with Alma. She couldn't know anything about any other suspect."

"Look here, Norris, you'll have to remember that I'm out to find the murderer of Sampson Tracy. I'm not considering whether the evidence I collect is going to implicate this one or that one, or whether it isn't. I want only the truth."

"Well, I don't," I told him. "I want to clear Alma Remsen, and I'd perjure myself straight into perdition if it would do her any good."

"Well, it wouldn't. Your word, after that speech, isn't worth the effort it takes to speak it, as you must see for yourself. Why don't you try to realize that that sort of talk won't get you anywhere, nor help the girl either. Why don't you try to understand that to find the real murderer is the only thing to free Miss Remsen, and the only way to do that is to investigate."

All of a sudden, I saw myself for a silly fool.

"You're right, March," I said, earnestly; "and I'm going to try."

"That's more like it," he applauded. "Come on, we'll work together."

144

CHAPTER XVII

AMES TAKES A HAND

"I've just read a detective story, where a sweet young girl was the criminal, after all," Maud said, contributing an argument to our conversation.

It was Sunday, the day after the Tracy funeral.

As we sat on the porch, after the midday dinner, Ames came along and joined our group.

"Well, Mr. Moore," he said, "unless you consider yourself engaged by me on the Tracy case, and you certainly have never given me to understand that, I am ready to call the deal off."

"Why?" Keeley said, offering him a cigar.

"Principally because the evidence seems so strong against Alma Remsen, and I've no wish to see that girl convicted."

"Why not?"

"First, because she isn't guilty, and second, because, if she were guilty, I don't want to be in any way instrumental in bringing it home to her."

"You'd compound a felony——"

"Oh, rubbish! But, yes, of course, I'd compound a felony rather than raise a finger to help establish her guilt."

"What makes you think she is guilty?"

"I didn't say I thought she was guilty, I said the evidence seems to point that way. But evidence doesn't always point to the truth, by any means."

"Very true. Have you any other suspect?"

"I'm not looking for suspects. I want to get away from the whole business."

"Yet only a few days ago, you wanted me to investigate this matter at your direction and at your expense."

"I know it. But I've changed my mind. I want to go away, to go back home. If I'm needed for any purpose, you can always find me. I'm not going to disappear."

"I don't think you'll be wanted by the authorities, Mr. Ames, if that's what you mean. I have crossed you off my list of suspects and I think Detective March has done the same. However, you will speak to them, of course, before you leave town."

"Oh, certainly. And, Mr. Moore, I've been doing a bit of looking about on my own. I don't know that it will be of help or even interest to you, but I've satisfied myself that nobody at Pleasure Dome was the murderer of Sampson Tracy."

"You mean no member of the household?"

"Yes, none of the staff of servants, neither of the secretaries, nor myself. That completes the tale of the occupants of the house that night."

"And how have you come to your conclusions?"

"By questioning, both straightforward and also more adroit. I have talked to the servants, and I have examined their rooms and possessions, and I have no hesitancy in pronouncing them all innocent."

"Perhaps they know something about it, though."

"Not the ones who are there now. A few, I believe, have been dismissed. They may know something. I cannot get at them, of course. But those who are there, and they are the principal ones, are innocent, and are eager to find the criminal."

"They do not, then, suspect Alma Remsen? Surely they would not be anxious to discover her guilty."

"No, they will hear no word against her. Griscom, especially, flies into a rage at a hint of her implication in the matter."

"And the two secretaries?"

"Are as innocent as I am. I can scarcely expect you to take my word about myself, but I want to witness for Everett and Dean. They had no reason to kill Tracy, for I don't agree that their expected legacies were sufficient motive. I had a motive, I suppose, as I sorely needed the money he left me, but I didn't kill him to get it."

Ames didn't smile, he made his statement in a calm, honest way that carried absolute conviction. And there was no evidence against Ames. Had he wanted to kill Tracy, he surely would not have gone to the trouble to fix up all those foolish decorations, nor would he have been apt to think of making that telltale scratch across his own door.

"I think nobody suspects you, Mr. Ames," Keeley said, and Ames returned:

"No, nobody does. They're all on the trail of Alma Remsen. By all, I mean of course, the police; there's nobody else sleuthing, that I know of, except yourself."

"There is plenty of evidence that seems to point to Miss Remsen," Kee said, slowly, "the question is, does it really indicate her? Did you ever hear, Mr. Ames, that she was in any way affected, either physically or mentally, by any disorder that would make her—er—irresponsible in her behaviour?"

Ames moved uncomfortably in his chair.

"I'd rather not answer that question," he said, "but I suppose my disinclination to reply would be construed as affirmative. So,

146

while I decline to discuss it, I will admit that I have heard rumours to that effect."

"Then if it can be proved that she is mentally affected, surely no punishment can come to her, even in case of conviction."

"Perhaps not. But if she is mentally afflicted, it seems all the more horrible to add to her sufferings the horrors of a trial."

My heart warmed toward Harper Ames. At least, he had the instincts of a human being, and not those of a cold-blooded sleuth.

"You feel, as I do, that the bizarre effects of that deathbed implies, or at least suggests, the work of a disordered mind?"

"Either that, or an exceedingly clever mind trying to give the effect of a more or less demented person."

"Have you, in your talks with the servants or secretaries, learned any rational explanation for those strange conditions?"

"None at all."

"One more question, please, Mr. Ames," Kee said, gravely, "and then I have done. Have you, since the death of Sampson Tracy, learned of any incident aside from these strange conditions we have mentioned, that seems to you to implicate Miss Remsen?"

An obstinate look came over Ames's face, and he shook his head, but it was plain to be seen that he was concealing something.

"You can't expect us to believe that half-hearted negation," Kee said, with a nod of understanding. "I know you don't want to accuse that poor girl of anything more, but try to realize that what you think against her interests may be for them."

"That's a new way to put it!" and Ames looked a little bewildered. "But it might be true. You know in the story books the nephew is always overheard having a violent altercation with his uncle, but he is always proved innocent."

"Who overheard Miss Remsen quarrelling with her uncle?"

"I did. I may as well tell you, for I daresay it is my duty. And it may, as you say, redound to her favour, though I can't see how. Well, I was passing through the hall on the Tuesday afternoon, the afternoon she said she was there, you know, and the two were in the library. The door was partly open, and with no intent of eavesdropping, I couldn't help hearing some words as I went by. Alma was talking, and while not loud, her voice was strained, tense, as if with deep feeling or passion. She was saying: 'Please don't tell Mrs. Dallas, uncle, please don't! If you do, I shall do something desperate! I can't bear it to have you tell her! She hates me, anyhow, and it would make her hate me worse! Uncle, I beg of you....' I heard no more, as I went right along."

"You're sure of what you did hear?"

"Sure of the intent. I may not have the words exact. But Alma was very angry and Tracy very decided. I gathered that. And the speech I heard was absolutely as I have told you in meaning, if not in identical language."

"Well, let's come right down to it. You think Tracy proposed to tell his prospective bride that his niece had an affliction that made her uncertain of herself at times?"

"That is what I think. I know that Tracy planned to tell Mrs. Dallas something—and you know she declared that herself—so, hearing Alma say what she did, how can one help putting two and two together?"

"It may be as you say. But what about the theory that Alma is shielding somebody?"

"Who can it be? Only one or both of those strange old people who take care of her. And somehow, I can't see her running her own head into a noose to save them, even if they are in danger, which, by the way, I haven't heard that they are."

"They're not definitely suspected that I know of, but I've thought it might be that they were so upset by Tracy's determination to expose the secret of Alma's affliction, that one of them might kill him to prevent such a disclosure."

"Ingenious as a theory," Ames said, "but not very probable as I see it."

"Why not?"

"First of all, would either of those people, capable of murder though they might be, cut up all those monkey-tricks that looked like the work of a diseased mind? Just the way to draw suspicion on their beloved charge."

"That's a facer," Kee agreed, "unless they didn't think of that, and only arranged the flowers and things with a view toward general bewilderment."

"Not good enough. No, Alma isn't shielding anybody, but she is queer, very queer. And the older servants, Griscom and Fenn, are worried sick about her."

"They don't believe she did it?"

"They don't know what to believe. There's so much against the girl. And there's a rumour that somebody saw her over there that night."

"Who saw her?"

"I can't find out. One maid told me another maid had told her so, but Fenn came along and gave the girl a dressing down, and she won't open her lips now."

"Well, Mr. Ames, I'm grateful for the facts you have detailed. Every fact helps, just as every opinion hinders. Isn't Miss Remsen now the owner and head of the Pleasure Dome estate?"

"In a way, yes. Legally, of course, she is the rightful heir. And as she is not under arrest, she can take possession if she chooses. But she says she won't go there until this inquest matter is over, and then, I suppose if she should be accused and arrested, the place would be shut up for a time."

"Hard lines on Mrs. Dallas," Maud said, "losing her expected fortune and prominent position."

"Yes, and no." Ames smiled a little. "Between you and me, Mrs. Merrill, though Mrs. Dallas is terribly shocked at the manner of his death, I can't feel she is mourning deeply for Mr. Tracy. I think Charlie Everett had pretty well cut out the elderly millionaire."

"Well, that's her business," Lora said, coldly. "I am so sorry for Alma, I've no sympathy to spare for Mrs. Dallas. They can't arrest the girl if she isn't responsible for her actions, can they?"

"I don't know. It depends on conditions and circumstances."

"I hope, Mr. Ames," I said, speaking more pleasantly than I felt, because I had no wish to antagonize him, "that you won't feel it necessary to tell any one else what you have told us. Mr. Moore, of course, will tell the police whatever he deems wise, but I mean the matter needn't become village gossip."

"No, Mr. Norris," Ames returned. "I have no wish to have Miss Remsen's name bandied about. And now that I have told all I know, my own conscience is clear, and if not detained by the authorities, I shall go home. But I daresay they will keep me until after the finish of the inquest on Friday."

Ames went off and his departure was closely followed by the arrival of that detestable little Posy May.

I cordially disliked the girl, and I felt sure she was bringing fresh tales about Alma.

Nor was I wrong.

The flapper swung herself over the arm of a big chair, and landed Turkish fashion in its depths. Demanded cigarettes and their attendant paraphernalia.

Then, with a solemn, owl-like expression on her pert little face, she said, "I have additional information."

Keeley prepared to listen, for he had often said he gained more knowledge from outsiders than from the regular force.

"Yes," Posy went on, "I've been inquiring round among the folks who live nearest to Whistling Reeds Island, and I've found three who have seen Alma when she was in her tantrums."

"Look here, Miss May," I said, hoping to trap her, "how is it that you or your friends you've been interviewing can see what goes on on the Island? I've been there, and it seems to me it's so walled in by trees and shrubs that there's little visible from the lake."

"That's true, Mr. Norris," Posy spoke seriously, "but there is a place at the back of the house, a sort of vista, small, but open. I think somebody removed a tree or two in order to see out. If your boat is in line with that, you can see in quite plainly. That's where I saw Alma when she was paddywhacking the old nurse, and that's where my friends have seen exhibitions of the same sort."

Posy had a quaint way with her, when she was serious, and somehow she gave the impression of sincerity in what she said.

Anyway, she had the attention of her hearers and she went on, excitedly:

"So, I asked the girls, and they couldn't remember at first, and then the three of them said yes, they had seen Alma through that opening in the trees. And they said—one of them did—that she saw Alma going for the nurse with a croquet mallet. And the man—that's the nurse's husband—had to come and pull Alma off of his wife!"

"Now, Posy," Kee looked at her sternly, "I don't want these yarns at all if there's a bit of fairy story about them. Do you know them to be true?"

"I honestly think so, Mr. Moore, because I made Ethel—it was Ethel Wayne who told me this one—cross her heart and hope to never if it wasn't true. And Ethel is a truthful girl, anyway. Why, once she——"

"Never mind side shows. Now, if you feel certain you have true stories to tell, get on with the others. Who next?"

"Oh, you hurry me so! Well, then I struck Mary Glenn. She is a very serious thinker, and she wouldn't exaggerate a tiny mite, she wouldn't. And she said she saw something she never had told anybody, not even her mother. And she wouldn't tell me at first, till I told her it was official work I was doing and that if she didn't tell I'd set the force on her. You know everybody is quelled at mention of the law and so she came off her perch, and told me."

"Told you what? Now, repeat it as she said it, don't embroider it any."

"No, sir. Well, she said she saw Alma through that same gap in the hedge, and Alma wasn't angry or anything like that, but she was throwing things into the lake. And the nurse was trying to stop her, but she couldn't. Alma threw in her string of beads and then her hat and then her slippers and then a book she had with her, and then something else, Mary couldn't see what that was. And all the time the nurse was saying, 'Now, Miss Alma—oh, please be good, Miss Alma,' and like that. So, if Alma Remsen isn't off her head, I don't know who is!"

"You said there were three," Moore said, quietly, "go on, please."

"The last is the strangest of all," Posy said, with a tense calm, quite like Keeley's own. "Daisy Dodd told me, and she's a most reliable person. I'd trust Daisy to tell the truth about anything! Well, she was out in her canoe, one afternoon, late, you know, about dusk, and she saw Alma come out through that gap in the trees, and stand on the edge of the lake. It's awful deep there, and there's quite a high bank. Well, Alma stood on the bank, and all of a sudden she put up her hands, and splash!—she dove in! Daisy was scared to death, it was so deep and all, but Alma came right up, and swam off a few strokes and then she swam back to shore, and scrambled up the bank, all dripping wet."

"Had she on a bathing suit?"

"No, that's just it. She had on her everyday clothes, one of those sports suits she 'most always wears, and she came out of the water, like a drowned rat, and then stood, looking at herself as if surprised she should have done what she did."

"Was the nurse on the scene that time?"

"Daisy said, she rowed on then, but as she was nearly past, she heard somebody cry out, 'Oh, Miss Alma, what have you been up to?'"

"Well, Posy, is that all?"

"Yes, Mr. Moore, and you can depend on it all as being true, at least so far as I know. And I know those girls would never make up those yarns, there'd be no sense in that, would there?"

"No, I can't see that there would," Keeley said, speaking absent-mindedly as if his thoughts were on the stories he had just heard.

"Posy, you're a good girl," Lora said, feeling, I was sure, that somebody ought to give the girl the applause she had earned. "But you're going to keep those things secret for us, aren't you?"

"Yes'm, I'm going to do just what you and Mr. Moore tell me. For I've made up my mind. I've found myself and I'm going to make detective work my vocation. I think I have a decided talent for it, and I am sure——"

"Well, Posy," Keeley said, suddenly waking up, "if you want to be a detective one of the first things to learn is to keep your mouth shut. Can you do that?"

"Yes, sir. I've just promised Mrs. Moore not to say a word until you say I may."

"That's a good girl. Now if that finishes your report, I'll excuse you for to-day. I have to act upon your information, you know. You feel sure, don't you, that these episodes happened just as you've narrated them?"

"Yes, I do. I know those girls, and what they say they saw, they saw. Daisy said she thought Alma was a little lacking, but the others didn't say that, they only thought she had a fierce temper that broke out suddenly sometimes."

"Either of those things may be true, but don't think about it. Run off now, and play with your sheik. And forget all about this case unless you get some further knowledge that is both true and important. But, remember, not a word of it to any one—not any one at all!"

"See my finger wet, see my finger dry, see my finger cut my throat if I tell a lie," said the girl, in a singsong tone, and with accompanying dramatic gestures of fearful histrionic fervour.

Then she ran away, and we sat and looked at one another.

"The problem seems to be solved," I said.

"Seems to be," Moore returned, and something in his voice gave me a grain of hope. I don't know what it was, it was not really encouragement, but I knew he had a ray of light from somewhere, and I had to be content with that.

"You believe all Posy said, don't you, Kee?" Lora asked.

"Yes, I do. Those youngsters aren't going to make up such things, and I know that gap in the line of trees, I've often looked in there but I never had the luck to see any drama enacted."

"Why do they have that break when they seem so anxious for utter concealment?" Maud inquired.

"Maybe the servants cut it for convenience in taking in parcels, or to look for their sweethearts," Kee surmised. "Oh perhaps it just happened that a couple of trees died and haven't yet been replaced. I say, Gray, why don't you go over to see Alma?"

I nearly fell off my chair at this, and my heart bounded at the idea. Then, I thought what it might mean, and I said, bitterly:

"To spy on her, and come home and tell you what I've ferreted out?"

"I feared you'd say something like that," he returned, gently. "But while you can do that or not, as you choose, I tell you honestly, I had only your own interest at heart When I suggested it."

"Then I'll go," I said, heartily, knowing Kee incapable of insincerity.

"What are you going to give as a reason for calling?" Lora asked, smiling kindly at me.

"The truth," I said, smiling back, and in a few moments I was off.

I jumped into a rowboat, a canoe was not such a familiar craft to me as to the others, and I rowed away to the island house.

The dour boathouse keeper met me, and after a mere word of greeting I hurried up the path to the house.

Merry herself answered my ring, and at first she looked stern and unapproachable. "Miss Alma is seeing nobody, sir," she informed me. "She is lying down just now."

"Won't you ask her if she couldn't give me a few minutes? I'm not here on business of any sort, I'm just making a social call, and perhaps I can cheer her up."

I had unwittingly struck the right note, for Merry smiled a little, though the tears came into her eyes, too, and she gave me a long look as she said, "sit on the porch, please, sir, and I'll ask Miss Alma."

I sat down, and there, in that strange, eerie stillness, in that quiet, mysterious atmosphere, I vowed my life to Alma Remsen, I consecrated my heart and soul to my darling, and I determined to save her from this cloud that seemed to hang over her.

To be sure, my ideas of this salvation and indeed of the cloud itself were a trifle vague, but both mind and soul were full of her and her dearness, and at a light step behind me I turned to see her coming toward me across the verandah.

All in white, her golden curls a little tumbled, and her big, beautiful eyes a little heavy with trouble and sadness, she came, her two hands outstretched as if asking my aid.

I rose slowly, as she slowly advanced, and it seemed to me that as she traversed those few feet across the porch and as I awaited her, we asked and answered all the necessary questions, and when at last I held her two dear hands in mine, I drew her nearer into my arms and clasped her to me.

She made no resistance, she did not hold back or repulse me, but lay against my breast like a tired child, finding haven at last.

I held her so, soothing her a bit, and caressing her golden head, but saying no word lest I startle her.

In a moment, she lifted her head, her eyes gazed into mine and all the woe and sorrow came back into them.

"No, dear," I said, "no, don't look like that. Look happy——"

"Happy!" she said, with an awful intonation.

"Yes," I said, "like this!" and I kissed her.

CHAPTER XVIII

ALL RIGHT AT LAST

It was just after I had given Alma that first kiss, and had realized that she was not offended by my daring, that Merry came to the house door, crying out, "Come, Miss Alma, come quickly!" and with an agonized look, Alma begged me to go at once, and she herself ran into the house.

Then John Merivale came out and controlling his agitation with an effort, he said, "If you please, sir, Miss Remsen asks that you go home now. She cannot see you again and she will send you some word later on."

"Tell me what's the trouble, Merivale," I urged. "I am a friend of Miss Alma, more than a friend, indeed."

I looked at him squarely, as man to man, and he gazed back at me, his face drawn with strong emotion of some sort.

"If you want to help her, sir, you'll just go quietly away. You can do nothing here."

So, there was nothing to do but to go, and I started off down the garden path.

I looked back at the house as I stepped on the dock, but I saw nobody at any window, nor any sign of anybody about.

It was all mysterious, terribly so, but I had the remembrance of that moment when I had held Alma close in my arms, and she had offered no resistance.

Surely, some day, the clouds would clear away and all would be explained.

Slowly I rowed back to the Moore cottage and pondered as I went.

When I reached Variable Winds, I found the family and Detective March in full conclave.

Spread on a table before them lay a conglomerate collection of small objects, among which I recognized a lot of beads that I had seen Alma wear, a pretty finger ring and several other odd bits of jewellery. Also, some scraps of bright coloured silk, that I felt, intuitively, were bits of the Tracy waistcoats. Also, a Totem Pole, broken into three pieces.

I sat down with the others, and prepared to enter the discussion.

"I want to know all about it," I said. "All you know. Don't keep anything back with the idea of sparing my feelings. I have not had a definite talk with Alma, but I have reason to think she cares for me, and I am content to bide my time. But, I propose to do all I can to save her from what I feel sure is a mistaken suspicion of her guilt in the Tracy matter."

"Very well," said March, looking at me gravely, "then please understand that the evidence against Miss Remsen is overwhelming. You know most of it, you have heard nearly all the details of the case as they have come to light. Now, try to realize that the cumulation of all these facts is a mountain of proof that will be hard to move."

"I have heard it stated," I said, calmly, "that circumstantial evidence, though seemingly convincing, must never be taken as absolute proof."

Keeley stared at me, as if amazed, but I stood my ground.

"You'll have to get a human witness before you can declare a certainty."

"True enough, Mr. Norris," March agreed. "And we have plenty of human evidence. Mr. Ames's story of the quarrel between Miss Remsen and her uncle, you have heard. At that time Miss Remsen declared she would do something desperate, if Sampson Tracy persisted in his determination to tell Mrs. Dallas something that Alma wanted kept secret. What could that be, save the fact of her own defective health, or impaired mentality? She said Mrs. Dallas already hated her, and, knowing that, would hate her more. What other construction can possibly be put on those words? Then, we have Jennie's story of Miss Remsen's behaviour the night of Mr. Tracy's death. That girl would never invent a story so wildly improbable as the tale of Miss Remsen jumping from the window into the lake."

"You'll have to admit all March says is true, Gray," Keeley said to me, his fine face drawn with deepest concern. "And also the stories Posy May has told us. They bear the stamp of truth, and they are all human evidence, not merely circumstantial. Now, I will tell you the conclusion that I have been obliged to arrive at. And that is, that Alma Remsen is indeed afflicted. Not with epilepsy but with a far more serious malady. I mean dementia praecox. This is a terrible statement to make, but I am sure it is the only diagnosis that fits the case. As you may or may not know, that condition may be in existence yet remain unknown and unsuspected by those nearest and dearest to the patient."

"No!" I cried, recoiling from the thought of horrors that this idea conjured up. "That lovely girl——"

"You know nothing about the disease, Gray," Keeley said, patiently. "I didn't know much about it myself, until I read it up,

155

which I have just done. It has many forms and phases, but there are some symptoms inseparable from the conditions. For instance, and this is the thing that impressed me from the very first. You remember I said the watch in the water pitcher was the keynote. Well, I had a vague idea, and my recent study has corroborated it, that victims of this dread disease almost invariably throw a watch into a jar or pail of water if they get a chance. That is a common peculiarity, and all the queer work around Tracy's deathbed points unmistakably to a mind disordered by dementia praecox and nothing else. Epilepsy won't do. That is a different disease. But the feather duster, the flowers, the waistcoat business, the Totem Pole, and more than all, the fatal nail, all indicate the same thing. Now, this disease has the strange quality of becoming evident at times, and then disappearing so utterly that no one would suspect its presence in the person affected. March and I have concluded that Alma Remsen is a victim of this horrible curse and that her actions are in no way of her own volition during the attacks of the dementia."

"I can't believe it," I said, after a straight glance into Keeley's sympathetic eyes, "but I suppose I must take your word for it. However, it makes no difference in my love and loyalty to Alma, but I want to get at the truth. Now if it is true, her doctor must know about it. And I can't think Doctor Rogers would have gone off and left her if there was danger of attacks of such a sort."

"That's the way it seemed to me," Keeley said. "Now, listen, Gray, and we'll tell you all. We have tried to think Alma is shielding somebody, somebody maybe that is a victim of dementia praecox. We thought of the two Merivales and we considered their daughter, Dora. Any of the three are possible, you see. Then, owing to some things March noticed when making his search at Whistling Reeds, we had a new suspicion. He observed two breakfast trays, in the pantry cupboard, that had the general effect of being in frequent use and the dining table was used for two. He observed a can of cocoa, though he had been told that Miss Remsen had always coffee for her breakfast. He thought the guest room showed signs of being in use when there was no acknowledged company there. Indeed, he brought that lot of stuff on the table from the guest room waste basket. As you see, there are bits of jewellery and a lot of beads and such odds and ends. Those are the things a demented person throws away. Also, there are bits of the waistcoats that have been so much talked about. Well, we came to the conclusion that there was another inmate of that house beside Alma Remsen. Some relative or friend she was shielding, or perhaps the nurse or her daughter. Again, it might be a man, say, an unacknowledged brother or cousin, whose very existence had been kept secret. Anyway, there was a very decided mystery to be unravelled at Whistling Reeds. But then, Posy May's stories and Jennie's, too, brought it all back to Alma herself, and while we hated to do it we had to find out. And the surest way was through Doctor Rogers. So I telegraphed him at a dozen or more different places where he might possibly be found, and one of them hit its mark."

Keeley drew a telegram from his pocket and passed it over to me. It sounded cryptic, for it ran thus:

YES A R VICTIM OF D P RECORDS IN MY SAFE LINCOLN
HOLDS KEY

"And so," March said, rising, "we are just going over to the office of Doctor Rogers to investigate the matter. You may go or not, as you wish."

"Don't go, Gray," Lora said, gently. "It is not necessary and will only cause you suffering. Keeley will tell you all when he comes back. You stay here with me."

"Thank you, Lora, dear," I said, "but I must go. I must know every development as it takes place. I'm a little dazed with this news from the doctor, but I can't help feeling there's a mistake somewhere. It can't be that Alma——"

I stopped suddenly, for I remembered seeing her on the lake that night, and hearing her say afterward that she never went on the lake in the evening. Then, when she had these attacks, she acted without knowledge of what she was doing. If she had, under these conditions, killed her uncle, she was of course in no way responsible, and would not be held so.

Maud and Lora looked sorrowfully after us, and we three went down the path to the drive and got into Keeley's car.

At Doctor Rogers's office we found his assistant in charge. He had but a few of the doctor's cases to look after and these were the simpler ones. Serious matters had been placed in the hands of more skilled practitioners, and some few important ones, we were told, were given over to specialists.

March showed him the telegram and asked what it meant.

"Well," said Doctor Greenway, a pleasant-faced young man, "I guess I can help you out on that. My orders are to meet the wishes of any one bringing a telegram couched in that language. As you have doubtless deduced," he smiled at the detective, "it means the key to the safe is hidden——"

"Behind Lincoln's picture," cried Kee, before March could speak.

"Yes," smiled the young man, his eyes following ours to the large engraving of Lincoln on the wall.

He stepped up on a chair, turned the frame from the wall a little, and from an envelope pasted on the back of the picture he extracted a paper.

"This is the combination," he explained, "which is what he means by key."

Following the message on the paper, he twirled the dials, and soon opened the safe.

"I will leave you to your investigations," he said. "This must be an important matter, or Doctor Rogers wouldn't have sent that information. Those are his case books, I leave them in your charge. When you are finished with them I will return and close the safe again. I shall be in the next room."

He went out and closed the door, and we looked into the safe, wondering what secret it would divulge.

So well was everything labelled and indexed that we had no trouble at all in finding the pages marked Remsen.

Keeley and March did the research work, I sitting idly by, but alert to learn their findings.

In a moment, I saw the utmost surprise and excitement manifest on their faces. They read from the same page, silently, eagerly, and then Keeley lifted his head, and with a look of pure joy on his face cried out:

"Take heart, Gray, Alma is all right!"

My heart almost stopped beating. I couldn't speak, but my whole soul seemed to go out in a great prayer of gratitude that swallowed up all other emotion. I did not hasten them or beg for further disclosures; I knew they would come in good time.

At last they gave over reading and turned to look at one another with nods of understanding.

Then Keeley turned to me, and said, concisely:

"Gray, the dementia praecox patient is not Alma, but her sister—her twin sister, Alda. This twin did not die as a child, but lived, afflicted with this terrible disease. The mother of the little girl was so overcome with grief and shame, that she pretended the child had died, and had the little grave made to give credence to the story."

"Alda?" I said, dully, not quite taking it in. "That isn't a name—"

"It is the name of Alma's twin, anyway," March said, grasping me by the shoulder, none too gently. "Wake up, man, you have something to live for now! Listen to me. Alma's twin sister is in the house at Whistling Reeds, and has been there all the time. While their mother was alive she kept the girls at Pleasure Dome, Alma

158

openly and Alda secretly. No one knew of the sister's existence except the three Merivales and Griscom and Mrs. Fenn.

"They were bound to secrecy by Sampson Tracy, and he knew how to command obedience. Of course, Tracy and Alma knew all. Then, when Alma's mother died, she left Alda as a sacred trust, and Alma has devoted her life to the afflicted twin. You see, Alda is normal and sane the greater part of the time. But she cannot be allowed to know people for there is no telling when the spasms will come on. And when they do there is no treatment necessary save to control and soothe her. The Merivales, with Alma, look after that, and much of the time the two girls are together."

"Now, you see the truth of March's deductions that there was another inmate of the Whistling Reeds' house," Keeley said. "Where they keep her, I don't know, but——"

"Let's go right over there," March suggested. "It's only fair to end Miss Alma's misery and suspense as soon as possible."

Still dazed and wondering, I watched the others recall Doctor Greenway and give him back the paper he had produced, and then we went away—back to Keeley's place, and into a boat and over to Whistling Reeds with all possible speed.

The glum boatmaster greeted us surlily, as usual, but March paid no attention and made straight for the house.

His ring was answered by Merry herself, and she looked very perturbed and anxious.

"I'm glad you've come, gentlemen," she said. "We are in great trouble."

It was then that I took the helm. As Alma's fiancé, for I so considered myself, it was my right and my duty to take matters in charge.

"Mrs. Merivale," I said, simply, "we know all about Miss Alda."

She staggered back a step and then a look of relief passed over her strong, gaunt face.

"Yes, sir," she said, apparently accustomed to accept the word of her superiors. "Then you can advise us, sir. Miss Alda is took very bad."

"Do you want a doctor?" asked March, hurriedly.

"No, sir, a doctor can do nothing—nothing at all."

"What can we do?" Keeley asked, eagerly.

"I don't know yet—perhaps if you'd just wait down here, till I see how she is now——"

"Merry," called a man's voice from upstairs, and she hurried away.

I recognized the tones of John Merivale and I did not offer to go upstairs with the nurse, knowing she would call us, if necessary.

I longed to be with Alma, to comfort and care for her, but I could not intrude uninvited.

But after we had waited perhaps a half hour, Alma came downstairs and out to the porch where we sat.

She was composed, but with a new sadness in her eyes and a new droop to her lovely lips.

"I will tell you all," she said, quietly, as she sat down, opposite to the three of us. "Since you know of my sister's existence, there is no more occasion for secrecy."

"Take it easy, Miss Remsen," said March, with well-meant kindness, and Keeley rose, and then went and sat beside her.

I had an instant's flash of jealousy, then realized it was better so. This ordeal had to be gone through with, and were I near her, I should have been unable to resist the impulse to clasp her in my arms in spite of the others' presence.

Kee seemed to give her courage by his sympathy, and she began her story.

"I am so alone," she prefaced it, "that I must tell it all in my own way. It is a strange story, but here are the facts. When my sister and I had scarlet fever, she did not die, but she at that time began to show symptoms of dementia praecox. My mother learned this, and knew the inevitable progress and end of the malady. So she declared that her little girl was dead to her and dead to the world, and should remain so, apparently. She therefore, with the knowledge and permission of Uncle Sampson, pretended that the child had died, and ever after kept her hidden from all but the few servants who knew about it. Uncle Sampson was very kind; I learned later that he thought my mother demented also and that's why he humoured her so. But she was not, Doctor Rogers will tell you that. The years went by, and while my mother made a pretense of sorrowing for her dead child and often visited the little grave, she had great solace in taking care of my twin, Alda, and doing everything to make her life happy and pleasant. At Pleasure Dome, the grounds and house are so enormous it was not difficult to keep up the pretense and all went well until my mother died. As she left Alda to me, with an injunction to guard her as my life, I have tried to do all I could to obey her wishes. And I managed beautifully until Uncle Sampson wanted to marry and bring a wife home. There was only one thing to do, so we did it. I moved over to this secluded spot, and lived here, keeping Alda's existence still a secret. The trouble came when Uncle Sampson determined to tell Mrs. Dallas about Alda. Uncle thought it dishonourable not to tell her, and I feared if she knew it, the secret would be a secret no longer. Uncle and I quarrelled about this, the last time I ever saw him."

160

Emotion almost overcame Alma at this point, but she bravely controlled herself and went on.

"I told Merry about the quarrel, and Alda chanced to overhear me. You must realize that when she is not in the attacks of dementia she is as sane as you or I. But she got it into her head that Uncle Sampson had offended or injured me, and she resolved, I've learned from her since, that she would avenge that insult. Never before had she been inclined to homicidal mania, never did we think of her as becoming menacing or dangerous—Doctor Rogers would not have left her except that he thought she would go right along as she has been for years. A fit of fierce anger now and then, or a mad tempest of rage and foolish actions, always followed by a period of exhaustion and many days of languor. But this time, the disease took a new turn, and Alda went over to Pleasure Dome, taking my key to let herself in. Like all unbalanced brains, hers has a crafty slyness and she is very cunning when she wishes to be. She, I know now, for she has told me, read a story about a man who was killed by a nail driven in his head. Her poor, distorted mind chose to imitate that act, and she took with her a nail and a mallet. She did kill Uncle Sampson, as he slept, she put all those strange things round about him, she threw his watch in the water pitcher—she is always throwing things away—and then she took the waistcoats, which she coveted, for her fancy work, the Totem Pole, which she admired, and finding his door locked—she had locked it herself—she stepped up on the window sill and dived into the lake. She is a perfect mermaid in the water; she can dive anywhere and swim for any length of time and under any conditions."

"She had thrown out the waistcoats first?" asked March.

"Had she? I daresay. She was a little lame just then, having twisted her ankle a bit, but she swam to her canoe, got in it and paddled home in safety."

"You didn't miss her while she was absent?" Keeley inquired, interestedly.

"No, indeed. She hadn't been out at night lately, though at one time she did have the habit. She usually occupies the guest room, but when I have friends staying here, we keep her in a room in the third story. It is a pleasant room, but soundproof and securely barred. She was there during the funeral."

"Then you knew nothing of the tragedy until next day?"

"Nothing. And even then, when Mrs. Fenn called up and told me, I didn't think of Alda. I supposed it was heart failure or apoplexy. But when I learned of the nail I suspected the truth, and later, Alda told me all. She has no regret—I mean, her sense of right and wrong is so clouded now that she cannot think clearly. Her mentality has dwindled rapidly of late, and even now—she is sleeping after a sedative—I think she will not recover her mind to the extent of sanity she has shown of late. I'm not sure I am telling you this so you can understand it, but I am so stunned, so dazed to think the time has come to tell it, that I want only to tell it truthfully and all at once, I don't want to have to go over it again——"

Merivale appeared in the doorway.

"Miss Alma," she said, gravely, and in solemn tone, "Miss Alda is going."

Alma rose, not hastily, but with a sweet dignity, and turning to me, said: "Come with me, Gray."

It was like a chrism; I felt sanctified to be chosen to stand at her side in this supreme moment.

The others followed us, but I did not know it then.

Alma and I went up the stairs together and she turned toward the guest room.

There on the bed lay the counterpart of my own darling. I knew now that it was Alda whom I had seen that night in the canoe; it was Alda whom Posy May and her friends had seen in tantrums with the nurse, it was Alda who—poor demented, irresponsible child—had killed Sampson Tracy, in blind imitation of the story she had read about the nail.

She was beautiful, even as Alma was beautiful, but the light in her eyes was not the light of reason, rather the weird light of visions seen by a deficient mentality. But even as we looked, the restless eyes closed, the restless body subsided into stillness, and a coma set in, from which Alda Remsen never awakened.

We sent for a doctor, but there was nothing to be done, and though she lingered for two days, the spirit was at last set free, Alda was released, and Alma's long and ghastly term of servitude was over.

It has ever since been my pleasure and duty to bring only sunshine into that life that knew no real sunshine for many long years.

Alma felt she never wanted to see Pleasure Dome again, so the place was sold and we travelled in many lands, returning at last to found a home far removed from any memories of painful association.

The Moores are still our dearest friends, and the Merivales our staunch henchmen and caretakers; while Alma and I, sufficient to one another, take for our motto: "All for Love, and the World Well Lost!"

THE END

162